WAY TOO
MUCH
DRAMA

Earl Sewell

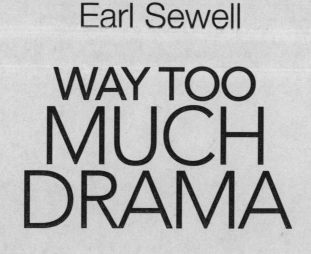

WAY TOO MUCH DRAMA

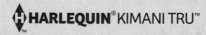
HARLEQUIN® KIMANI TRU™

Recycling programs
for this product may
not exist in your area.

ISBN-13: 978-0-373-53468-5

WAY TOO MUCH DRAMAA

Copyright © 2013 by Earl Sewell

This book is a work of fiction. The names, characters, incidents and places are the products of the author's imagination, and are not to be construed as real. While the author was inspired in part by actual events, none of the characters in the book is based on an actual person. Any resemblance to persons living or dead is entirely coincidental and unintentional.

For questions and comments about the quality of this book, please contact us at CustomerService@Harlequin.com.

® and TM are trademarks of Harlequin Enterprises Limited or its corporate affiliates. Trademarks indicated with ® are registered in the United States Patent and Trademark Office, the Canadian Trade Marks Office and in other countries.

Printed in U.S.A.

www.Harlequin.com

Dear Reader,

Please feel free to drop me a line at earl@earlsewell.com. Please put the title of my book in the subject line so that I know your message to me is not spam.

Make sure you check out www.earlsewell.net. You can also hit me up on Facebook at www.facebook.com/authorearlsewell and Twitter at www.twitter.com/earlsewell.

Earl Sewell

Children have never been very good at listening to their elders, but they have never failed to imitate them.
—James A. Baldwin

one

MAYA

"Hey, Maya. Snap out of it." Keysha popped her fingers a few times in front of my eyes before she placed her hands on my shoulders and shook me.

"You look like you're standing at the corner of Confused and Stunned. Is Viviana still on the phone?" Keysha asked. I had arrived at her house not too long ago and had been in the bathroom talking to her. Keysha had insisted that I come even though I'd injured my knee. I had gone to watch my ex-boyfriend, Misalo, fight Carlo, another guy I had sort of been dating. The fight had turned into an all-out brawl that involved everyone who had come to watch Misalo and Carlo beat each other senseless. My knee had gotten injured while running for safety when the fight got out of control.

"Hello? Why are you glaring off into space like a disoriented zombie?" Keysha clapped her hands several times.

I flinched and said, "I'm sorry." I placed my cell phone in my front pocket.

"Why didn't you confront Viviana on the phone about her wicked ways?" Keysha asked, as to why I had not forced my evil cousin, Viviana, to own up to what she had done.

Keysha and Viviana didn't exactly like each other, which

was cool with me because I hated Viviana more than saints despised sinners.

"She was being chased," I finally answered.

"Chased? By who?" Keysha asked as I thought about who'd want to beat Viviana down besides me.

"A group of girls. Through the park not too far from here. Viviana screamed into the phone and begged me to come and help, and then her phone died."

"Seriously?" Keysha's eyes questioned whether my words were true.

Nodding my head, I said, "Yeah." Then I glanced down at my knee, which was tender, so I began massaging it.

"Are you going to help her?"

I met Keysha's gaze and wondered why she had asked a question she already knew the answer to. I had absolutely no desire to aid my deceitful cousin.

Scrunching up my face as if I had suddenly caught the scent of a dead animal, I said, "No."

"You have to help." Keysha's insistence surprised me.

"What?" I shrieked, certain I had heard her wrong.

"We have to help her." Keysha spoke as if I had a moral obligation to do so.

"So let me get this straight. Thirty minutes ago you got into a scuffle with Viviana, and now that some other girls are about to beat her up, you want to go help her?" My words were filled with sarcasm. Keysha's harebrained idea was one for the books.

"I know I sound crazy, but I have my reasons for why I think we should lend her a hand."

"What you're saying doesn't sound crazy, Keysha. It sounds insane. Have you turned bipolar on me?" I gawked at her in frustration.

"Maya, listen." Keysha once again placed her hands on my shoulders, then met my gaze. "I know you're really ticked off with Viviana, and you have every right to be. Deep down you want to see her suffer for destroying your relationship with Misalo. Trust me, I get that."

"Viviana suffering isn't a harsh-enough punishment." I spoke from a bitterly cold place in my heart.

"I truly get it, Maya," Keysha repeated, trying to reassure me.

"Then why are you trying to convince me to help her?" I angrily asked. The very thought of Viviana brought my blood to a boil.

"Remember how much I used to hate Priscilla for ruining my prom dress, sleeping with my boyfriend and getting pregnant by him?" Keysha reminded me of some drama she'd had to deal with in her past.

"Oh, yeah. I'll never forget how you wanted to kill Priscilla on sight." A sour expression spread across my face.

"Remember how I was forced to save her life when she nearly drowned?" Keysha said.

I recalled the incident. Alex, an eighth grader who had a crush on Keysha, shoved Priscilla into the pool after she and Lori had tried to beat her up on the pool deck. Alex was only trying to help when he did it, but Priscilla could not swim and nearly drowned.

"I could've easily allowed her to die, but I set aside my animosity and did something I never thought I would do. I rescued her. I learned something when I did that," Keysha stated.

"Oh, really? What did you learn?" I asked, wondering what revelation she'd come to.

"Forgiveness, Maya. I had to forgive Priscilla before I

allowed myself to save her from certain death," Keysha whispered.

I raised my voice and said, "Well, I'm not ready to forgive that slut. She can burn in hell for all I care!"

"You don't mean that," Keysha said.

Refusing to take back my words, I said, "Yes, I do."

Keysha sighed disappointedly and asked, "Where did you say she was again?"

"At the park not too far from here. Why?" I asked, sensing that Keysha was about to do something foolish.

"I'm going to help her," she said, opening the bathroom door. Keysha walked out of the bathroom and I reluctantly followed. When we reached the family room, Keysha paused in front of her younger brother, Mike, who was sitting on the sofa texting.

"Mike, I need your help," Keysha interrupted him.

"How much money do you have?" Mike asked, momentarily glancing up from his cell phone.

"Okay, I need a favor then." Keysha rephrased her request for assistance.

"Girl, you know that I don't like handing out favors, especially to you." Mike once again began thumbing a text message.

"Stop being a jackass, Mike," Keysha snapped at him. Mike looked up. He glanced at me then back at Keysha. Sucking air between his teeth, he asked, "What kind of favor?"

"We need you to help us break up a girl fight," Keysha said in a hurried voice. "Now come on, before it's too late."

"Whoa! I like watching girl fights. I wouldn't want to break one up. I'm not the type of guy you need for that job. I will come along to watch, though," Mike said.

"You're such a typical guy. I don't even know why I bothered to ask you," Keysha fussed at her brother.

"You're starting to sound like Sabrina now. Nag, nag, nag, nag!" Mike spoke with a very annoyed voice.

"Whatever," Keysha said, then headed toward the door. I couldn't let her go alone so I trailed behind her.

"I swear, I don't see why or how Sabrina puts up with him," Keysha griped as we hurried to the park.

"Jeez! Would you slow down? My knee is killing me," I complained.

"I'm sorry," Keysha said, slowing down her hastened pace. At that moment, we were both startled by the sound of a car horn blowing beside us.

"Hey, I was just on my way over to see you, Keysha," said Wesley as he pulled up alongside us.

"When did you get a car?" I asked, admiring the cute white Volkswagen Jetta.

"It's my dad's. I have my license now, but I can only drive it locally," Wesley admitted.

"Good. Can you give us a ride to the park behind Maya's house?" Keysha asked.

"Yeah, hop on in." Wesley was more than willing to take us wherever Keysha wanted.

"What's going on at the park?" Wesley asked curiously. Wesley and Keysha used to date a long time ago. Now they were just good friends, although I got the feeling Wesley was interested in hooking back up with her.

"We're going to break up a fight," Keysha informed him.

"For real?" Wesley glanced over at Keysha as she got situated in the passenger seat. I was in the backseat admiring the interior of the car. The convertible top was down and the sun felt really good on my skin.

"I would look so cute in this car," I spoke aloud. I was hoping to distract Keysha and make her forget about assisting Viviana.

"Yeah, really," Keysha said as Wesley sped toward the park. He got us there in less than two minutes. When we pulled up, we didn't see Viviana or any other girls.

"The police probably came and broke it up already," I said with a sense of gratification. In my heart, I hoped Viviana was someplace unconscious with her nose smashed in dog crap. I was angry and that emotion gave my heart the permission it needed to blacken my thoughts, even if only for a moment. If I ever did see Viviana in a situation where she was injured and helpless, I knew I would be the first person to offer help.

"Pull over, Wesley," Keysha ordered. Once Wesley parked, the three of us got out of the car. We looked around, but saw no sign of Viviana or the pack of girls she claimed were attacking her.

"Is that her over there?" Wesley asked, pointing to a girl who was coming our way. She was cutting through the grass from the opposite side of the softball field.

"Yeah, that's her," I confirmed. She was walking lethargically. Keysha and Wesley began moving in her direction. I stayed put and rested my behind against the car.

"Are you coming?" Keysha looked over her shoulder at me.

"No. I told you my knee hurts." I offered up what I'm sure Keysha considered a lame excuse. I shifted my weight so that all the pressure was placed on my good leg.

"Maya, don't be like that. From what I can tell, it looks as if she could really use a hug."

"Fine," I agreed, walking with them.

As we approached, Keysha tried to hug Viviana to comfort her, but Viviana rejected her sympathy embrace.

"Get off me before I kick your butt," Viviana snarled at Keysha.

"You could at least say thanks to us for coming to help out," I scolded Viviana for being so ungrateful.

"I had it under control," Viviana answered stubbornly.

"From the look of things, I'd say you got your ass whooped," Keysha said.

"It's nothing. Just a ripped shirt, a few scrapes and messy hair." Viviana downplayed the degree of damage that had been inflicted upon her. Her long hair looked disheveled, and it was obvious that it had been yanked on several times during her scuffle.

"Your hand is bleeding." Keysha, still being kindhearted, reached for Viviana's hand.

"Hey! I said leave me the hell alone!" Viviana jerked away.

"Viviana, what the hell! She's only trying to make sure you're okay," I shouted at her.

"I don't need any help from either of you, okay! Just leave me alone!" Viviana yelled at the top of her voice as she moved on.

"Who were the girls that were chasing you?" asked Wesley.

"Why do you even care?" Viviana harshly glared at Wesley.

"You sound just as crazy as my ex-girlfriend, Lori," said Wesley unapologetically.

"Oh! Why do you want to bring that tramp up?" Keysha turned her attention to Wesley and awaited his response.

Lori was the reason she and Wesley had broken up.

"Uhm." Wesley paused, uncertain of what he'd done to

turn Keysha's aggression toward him. Boys can be clueless sometimes. The last name Keysha wanted to hear pass through Wesley's lips was Lori's, especially after Keysha had agreed to let him get close to her again.

"Her name shouldn't even be in your head, especially after the mess she put you through." Keysha didn't filter her words.

"Jeez, this is the second time I've tried to help a girl in need, thinking that I was doing the right thing. I'm never going to help out again because I only end up getting my head chewed off. Girls are way too complicated and love drama way too much. I swear, I feel like a cat chasing a red laser pointer whenever I try to figure girls out," Wesley said, washing his hands of the conversation. He turned and began heading back toward his car.

"Now do you see and understand how crazy Viviana is?" I looked at Keysha and waited for the acknowledgment that I was right all along and that we should've let Viviana deal with her own mess.

"Yeah, I see what you mean," Keysha admitted.

"She'll live," I said nonchalantly as I watched Viviana walking toward my house.

"Are you still going to talk to her about causing the breakup between you and Misalo?" Keysha asked.

"Don't worry. I'm going to deal with her in my own way," I said as I rested the palm of my left hand on Keysha's shoulder and hobbled back to the car where Wesley was waiting on us.

two

VIVIANA

MY body ached horribly. My right shoulder was throbbing because one of my attackers had bitten me. I had a headache because another one had pulled my hair. I also felt a lump swelling on my forehead, probably caused when someone nailed me with a dizzying hammer fist. It had been difficult to fight four girls at the same time, which felt like fighting a pack of wild dogs with my bare knuckles. They were able to throw four times as many punches, but a majority of their swings lacked accuracy. I was happy that I knew how to keep moving to dodge a total beat down. Still, for all the effort I had put into avoiding a punch, I had ended up taking a number of hits, but I'm tough like my father and can take punishment as well as dish it out. I bloodied the noses of two girls, and I'm certain that one of them will have a nasty-looking black eye thanks to my lightning quick right-handed jab. I don't know why they decided to beat me up. It could have been a random act, or, as I believe, a setup by my evil cousin, Maya. That's probably the reason she arrived so late after I had phoned her out of desperation and had begged her for help. I'll never do that again, ever.

When I arrived back at the house, I entered the kitchen through the patio door. My younger cousin, Anna, was in the kitchen making tamales. I'd walked in just as she placed some dried corn husks in a pot of boiling water. I knew that it would not be long before a delicious aroma would waft throughout the house. Anna did a double take as she casually glanced over her shoulder to say hello.

"Damn!" Anna blurted out.

"How bad do I look?" I asked, feeling the lump on my forehead getting tighter.

"Should I call nine-one-one? You look like you need a doctor," Anna said, turning off the stove. She hustled toward the refrigerator and removed an ice pack for my forehead.

"I don't need to go to the hospital. I'm fine," I assured her as she placed the cold ice pack against my skin.

"Did you get into a fight with Keysha and Maya again? If they did this to you, I swear, I'm calling Mom and Dad right now." Anna removed the ice pack and took a closer look at the swelling.

"I think Maya set me up, but I can't prove it," I uttered as I pulled back the fabric of my torn shirt from my right shoulder. "Is my shoulder bleeding?"

"OMG! Who bit you? These teeth marks look deep." Anna touched my shoulder as she continued questioning me.

"I don't know. Some chick," I answered as I pulled out a chair at the kitchen table and sat down.

"Was it Maya or Keysha who bit you?" Anna pulled up a chair and sat beside me.

"Anna, you must not have heard me. Neither Keysha nor Maya did this. Neither one of them were there. It was a group of girls who had been watching the fight between Misalo and Carlo. They started chasing me for no reason," I explained as I pulled off my gym shoes and ankle socks. I glanced at my sausage-shaped pale toes. They looked horrible and badly in need of a pedicure.

"I'm calling Mom." Anna reached for her cell phone.

"What good is that going to do, Anna? I don't even know who the girls are or what they looked like," I explained.

"Well, what if they jump you again? They could kill you, Viviana." I could tell by the tone of her voice that she was nervous and anxious.

"I doubt it. Beating me up wasn't as easy as they thought. I can handle myself," I said confidently. Anna hesitated for a moment. I could tell that she was trying to convince herself to not call her mother.

"The next time something like this happens, don't waste your time calling Maya. Call me. I'm not much of a fighter, but if the situation called for it, I'm pretty sure I can hold my own and help you out."

"I'll keep that in mind. How does my forehead look?" I asked.

"The swelling is going down," Anna said after taking another peek at my lump.

"I need a hot bath," I said as I rose out of my chair.

"Would you like for me to make you a tamale? You might feel better," said Anna.

"No. I'm not hungry right now. I'm going to take a bath, wash my hair and just chill out for a while," I said.

"Are you sure? My tamales are world famous," Anna said.

"Positive," I answered as I gingerly walked toward the staircase.

After taking a bath and washing the scent of sweat and grass out of my hair, I placed Neosporin on my skin scrapes and cuts and continued to place ice on my forehead. The knot had gone down considerably. I walked into the family room because I wanted to watch television. When I entered the room, Maya was already snuggled up on the sofa watching a romantic music video. She cut her eyes at me and then exhaled disgustedly.

"Do you have a problem?" I snapped, unmoved by her foul attitude about me.

"Yes, I have a big damn problem with you." Maya clicked off the television and folded her arms across her bosom.

"And I've got an even bigger problem with you. But that's not news to anyone," I said with just as much revulsion.

"Huh? I haven't done anything to you!" Maya growled at me. "But you! You're a tacky slut!"

"And you're a stuck-up, spoiled, delusional whore who doesn't know how to keep her mouth shut!" I barked back at her.

Maya rose to her feet and pointed an accusatory finger at me. "You purposely ruined my relationship with Misalo and I know it! I'll never forgive you for that."

"Ha! Your relationship wasn't all that damn strong. Misalo told me all about you and how you never truly appreciated him. He couldn't stand you and was going to break up with you anyway. I just took his blinders off so he could see how much of a sneaky tramp you are."

Maya opened her mouth so wide an airplane could have flown into it. "You're totally crazy. You actually believe all the crap that you tell yourself. You're mental."

"If telling the truth makes me mental, then so be it," I hissed at her. I felt my hatred for her swelling like a rising tide.

"You wouldn't know the truth if it came up and punched you on the nose. But that's okay. I'm not going to give you the satisfaction of ruining my life. I'm going to get Misalo back now that the truth has come out. I suggest that you stay away from him, unless you want something bad to happen to you!" Maya threatened me.

"Is that why you sent that pack of girls to beat me up? Huh? Come on, Maya, don't deny it," I said, forcing her to own up to what she had done.

"I didn't have a thing to do with that. Perhaps the girls just didn't like you. You have built up a reputation of being a backstabber," Maya said maliciously.

"And you have a reputation of being a snitch!" I reminded her of her soiled reputation with me.

"A snitch! Is that what this is all about? You still haven't gotten over that mess with your father?" Maya asked.

"You ruined my life, Maya, and I'll never forgive you for that. Had you kept your mouth shut, my father would be alive today, and I wouldn't have to live under the same roof with you! I hate the fact that you're alive, and I wish God would do the world a big-ass favor and strike you down!" Maya and I were now having a full-blown and very loud argument.

"Your father murdered someone!" Maya hollered at me.

"Were you there? Did you see him do it?" I pointed at her.

"No," Maya answered.

"Then how can you be 100 percent sure that he did it?" I cornered her with my question.

"I overheard him say what he'd done. You know that." Maya defended her justification for snitching on my father.

"You don't know what you heard, Maya. You've always had an overactive imagination and can't tell reality from fantasy. My father was the best man in the world. My life was perfect when he was alive. And you, with your lying-ass mouth, put an innocent man behind bars where he was killed. I hope you rot in hell, Maya."

"And I hope you burn in hell with your homicidal father!" Maya hobbled closer to me.

"You want a piece of me?" I asked as I balled up my fists and prepared to kick her butt.

"All you need to do is stay away from Misalo." Maya issued yet another warning as she limped toward the stairs.

"Why are you guys so loud? I can hear you all the way upstairs," said Anna, who had come to see what all the shouting was about.

"Viviana needs mental help," Maya hissed as she hopped up the steps.

"Wow! She's really pissed off," Anna said as she joined me in the family room.

"And I couldn't care less," I said as I settled into my seat. My head had begun to throb.

"I have a question I need to ask you." Anna pulled out her cell phone. "I just got a text about a fight between Carlo and Misalo. Did you see it? Do you know who won?"

"Does it really matter, Anna?" I answered, irritated.

"Yes. I want to know if Misalo kicked Carlo's butt. You were teaching him how to fight, right?" Anna asked.

"Yes," I answered.

"Well, did your man win or what?" Anna was eager to hear all the gory details.

"The fight didn't really last that long. Can we talk about it later? My head really hurts," I said.

"Would you like some aspirin?" she asked.

"Yeah," I said.

"Okay, I'll be right back," Anna said as she rushed off. I closed my eyes, exhaled and thought about what needed to be done in order to make Misalo care for me again. There was no way I would allow Maya to come between the true feelings that had developed between us.

three

MAYA

I was resting on my stomach when I was awakened by the sound of my cell phone. I wanted to ignore it, but I knew it was Keysha by the sound of the ring tone. Without looking, I reached for the nightstand where my cell phone was situated. Once I had it, I placed it to my ear.

"Hello?" I answered groggily.

"Wake up," Keysha said in a chipper voice. I closed my eyes tighter.

"What time is it?" I asked.

"It's time for us to get up and face the day," Keysha said energetically.

"Seriously?" I asked, annoyed.

"Stop acting like an old lady and wake up." It was obvious to me at that point that Keysha wanted me to do something with her.

"My knee still hurts. I'm not going to be out of bed anytime soon," I griped as I moved my injured leg.

"What if I told you that I got up first thing this morning and my dad took me to driving school?"

I perked up. "What?" I readjusted the phone. "Stop playing."

"I'm not playing," Keysha answered.

I turned over and looked at my alarm clock positioned on my dresser across the room. It was 12:45 p.m. "Wow! I didn't realize that I'd slept so late," I said, stretching out my body.

"You always sleep late when you're depressed," Keysha reminded me.

"I'm not depressed," I disagreed as I glared at the ceiling. I swallowed hard, noticing how dry my mouth was. "Are you really taking private driving lessons now?"

"Yep. I'm learning the rules of the road!" Keysha answered gleefully.

"Why didn't you tell me today was your first day? See, you're a crummy BFF. How could you keep something that major from me?" I asked.

"News flash! I was busy helping you deal with Viviana," Keysha answered sarcastically.

"That whore." I tossed my feet over the edge of my bed and sat upright.

"Did you get a chance to confront her about what she did?" Keysha asked.

"Oh, yeah. We had a big blowup yesterday after I got back home."

"And?" I could tell by the tone of Keysha's voice that she was hanging on my next words.

"She hates me, Keysha, and that's all there is."

"Does she hate you because of what went down with her father?" Keysha asked a question she already knew the answer to.

"Yep. She believes I ruined her life when I spoke up, and now all she wants to do is get even with me."

"Damn! How are you going to live under the same roof

with someone who has that much hatred for you?" Keysha asked.

"I have no idea," I admitted.

"You should probably tell your mom about it. Maybe she can help Viviana work through her issues," Keysha suggested.

"I care more about a baboon's smelly behind than I do about Viviana. All she has to do is stay out of my way and leave Misalo alone." My resentment toward Viviana was absolute.

"Speaking of feelings, boys and all that stuff, guess who I saw this morning?" Keysha asked.

"Wesley? Was he standing in the yard below your window reciting poetry?" I asked mockingly.

"No, silly, although that would be very romantic if he ever found the courage to do it." Keysha giggled.

"Oh, God," I responded as if I were about to puke.

"Whatever, Maya." Keysha chuckled. "I saw Carlo this morning."

"Carlo?" I spoke louder than I intended to.

"Yep."

"What was he doing?"

"I saw him walking into the community center. I assume he was heading to the gym. Have you spoken to him since the fight?"

"No. I haven't called him and he hasn't called me. He's probably ticked off at me for pulling him off Misalo when he was beating him down," I admitted.

"So does that mean you guys aren't an item anymore?" Keysha asked.

"I guess so. I'm not missing him at all, and he's certainly not chasing after me, so it is what it is," I answered as thoughts of Misalo filled my mind.

"Okay," Keysha said and then paused.

"What do you have planned for the day?" I asked.

"Right now I'm heading over to the library to return some books," Keysha said.

"The pool should be about to close for the season, shouldn't it?" I asked.

"Yep. I only have to work two more days and that's it," Keysha said.

"Well, at least you'll have plenty of money to do your back-to-school shopping with," I said, envious of the fact she had been able to work all summer.

"No, I have better plans for the money that I've been saving," Keysha said.

"What?" I asked.

"A car," said Keysha.

"You're going to spend all your money on a car? I thought you said your dad was going to buy you one?" I asked.

"That's what he said, but I don't want him to buy me some noisy jalopy. I've been able to save two thousand dollars. If he matches what I've saved, then I could get a decent vehicle for four thousand, don't you think?"

"Hell, yeah. You should be able to ride in style for that kind of money," I chimed.

"Do you want to head over to the library with me?" Keysha asked.

"Not right now. I need to stay off my knee for a little while longer. What are you doing later?" I asked, thinking we could do something then.

"I'll be at work," said Keysha.

"Then I'll come by the pool and keep you company later this afternoon," I said.

"Okay, I'll see you then," Keysha said before hanging up the phone.

Later that afternoon I put on my bathing suit, grabbed a pool bag, which I always kept packed and ready, and headed out the door. When I arrived at the swimming pool, Keysha was snapping off on some junior high school boys for playing too roughly. There was a mother with her toddler splashing around at the shallow end of the pool and a few other folks who were wading from one side of the pool to the other. I placed my things on an empty seat next to where Keysha's belongings were. I got myself situated, put on my dark sunglasses and relaxed. A few minutes later I felt someone shaking my shoulder.

"What?" I asked, annoyed by the interruption of my quiet time.

"Misalo just arrived," Keysha said, taking her seat beside me. I sat upright, and sure enough, Misalo had taken a seat at the other end of the pool.

"What are you going to do?" Keysha asked.

"I think I'm going to get in the water," I said. I rose to my feet and carefully walked to the edge of the pool. My knee was still bothering me a little, but not to the point that I had to hobble. I sat down on my butt, draped my legs over the edge and into the warm water. I splashed some water on my thighs and arms so my skin would adjust more easily to the temperature of the water. I then submerged myself. By the time I came from beneath the water, I noticed that Misalo wasn't in his seat. I glanced around, wondering where he'd gone. I looked below the surface of the water and saw that he was swimming toward me. I did a few strokes until my back rested against the edge of the pool. When Misalo surfaced, he cleared away the cascading water from around his eyes and approached me.

"Are you looking for me?" he asked, smiling innocently.

"I don't know. Should I be?" I asked, not willing to allow the charm of his smile to soften my disappointment in him, for not talking to me, not believing in me and instead listening to that liar Viviana.

"Where is your boyfriend?" he asked derisively.

"Where is your girlfriend?" I fired right back with an equal amount of sarcasm for his former boo thang, Viviana.

"Maya, I don't want to fight," Misalo said earnestly as his tone shifted.

"Ha! You should have thought about that before you started dating my cousin," I said.

"Oh, it's like that. I thought we could have a real conversation, but I see that I was wrong," he said and was about to swim away.

"I've been trying to have a real conversation with you for the longest time, but you've had your head up your butt." I didn't bother filtering my words.

"Okay, I'll give you that. I'll admit that I wasn't the easiest guy to talk to, but I'm certain you can see why I reacted the way that I did." Misalo gave me an innocent look.

"Misalo, you wouldn't even give me a chance to tell my side of the story," I said to him.

"I was angry, Maya," he admitted. "Sometimes when a person is angry, they can't see or think straight."

"And an angry person can be pretty stupid," I said, unwilling to soften my words or feelings.

"Whatever," Misalo said with lack of concern. It irritated me that he wasn't more apologetic.

"So do you want to hear the truth now? Or do you want to keep jumping to conclusions?"

"I don't think I jumped to conclusions. I believe the evidence I saw spoke for itself, at least in the beginning. Now I'm not really sure what to think. I'm confused," he admitted.

"You should've come to me for the truth instead of letting other people tell you their interpretation of what went down," I said.

"Okay, Maya. I get it. I should not have been so stubborn. Do you have time to tell me the truth now? What's really going on with you and Carlo?" he asked as he folded his arms across his chest and waited for me to explain my version of events. I paused momentarily and took notice of his muscles, which were much more defined. I exhaled before I began.

"Viviana and I snuck out of the house one night," I said.

"You snuck out of the house?" Misalo blurted out the words.

"I know, it's hard to believe, but, yes, I did. I was trying to prove to Viviana that I wasn't a Goody Two-shoes. Anyway, she knew about this party that was taking place in the city, so we hopped into my grandmother's car and went."

"You don't have a driver's license and neither does Viviana." Misalo immediately began questioning the credibility of my story.

"I know."

"That doesn't even sound like something you'd do, Maya. Besides, why would your grandmother give either one of you the keys to her car?" he asked.

"She didn't," I said, not wanting to admit that Viviana and I had pretty much taken the car for a joyride.

"You stole your grandmother's car?" Misalo's eyes widened as if he'd just been poked.

"Yes and no. Yes we took it, but we didn't steal it. Viviana said that she'd taken our grandmother's car lots of times."

"I don't believe a thing you're telling me, but go on," he insisted.

"It's the truth, Misalo."

"Maya, I've known you for a long time, and you've never done anything remotely close to what you're describing to me," he said as he repositioned himself next to me.

"It's the truth. You can even ask Keysha if you want," I suggested.

"Like she'd tell me everything. Keysha is your best friend and isn't going to admit to anything that would make you look bad."

"Keysha has no reason to lic, Misalo," I said as I scanned the pool deck. Keysha had climbed in the lifeguard chair. She'd put on her sunglasses and was keeping a close eye on everyone.

"Whatever," he said, dismissing my comment.

"So we get to this party and I don't know anyone there. I thought Viviana and I would use the time to bond, but she left me as soon as we arrived. I was nervous and afraid. As the night dragged on, I began searching for Viviana, but couldn't find her. It was then that I realized she'd set me up and left me. Her plan was for me to get busted for sneaking out of the house. Luckily, Carlo was there and offered to give me a ride home, but he wouldn't do it unless I slow danced with him first."

"Maya, your story sounds so lame." Misalo was skeptical. "If that's the case, how did Viviana tape you if she'd already left?"

"I don't know. Maybe I just didn't see her and she decided to record me," I said.

"Or, Carlo picked you guys up in his car and drove you there himself because you were creeping around with him behind my back all of the time." Misalo gave his own spin to the story.

"Misalo, stop making up stuff in your head that isn't true. I swear, that is not what happened." I attempted to put him back on the right track.

"You expect me to think that you actually snuck out of the house? I've asked you to do that for me countless times and you never would, Maya."

"I did it that one time, okay. It happened," I said more forcefully.

"Whatever," he said. I could tell that he didn't believe me.

"Now my turn," I said, turning the tables.

"Your turn?" Misalo seemed surprised that I had an issue with him.

"Yes. I have questions of my own for you," I said.

"I didn't do anything," he said.

"Ah, yes, you did. The photos that I sent to you. Why didn't you delete them? Why did you lie to me like you had? You've humiliated me, Misalo. So many guys have tried to have sex with me because of those photos."

"Okay, that technically wasn't my fault. I didn't really know that Viviana had gotten ahold of my phone and did that."

"Dude! You should have deleted the pictures. She would not have had anything to forward had you done what you were supposed to do," I raised my voice at him.

"I was stupid, okay. I never thought they'd ever leave my phone."

I shook my head disapprovingly at him.

"I'm sorry," he said. "I know I messed up."

His apology didn't seem sincere to me. I felt tears swelling. "Then you stooped so low by dating my cousin, Viviana. How could you even think that was cool?"

"It happened by accident," he said.

"By accident! Are you joking! Do you understand what you've done to me?" I angrily barked at him.

"You guys are getting a little too loud over here," Keysha spoke in a loud whisper as she walked past us. I had not noticed that she had come down from her perch.

"What was I supposed to think, Maya? Everything that I saw indicated to me that you and Carlo were an item. I even heard rumors that you and him had gone all the way."

"What! I can't believe you just said that to me. You should know me and know that rumor was a lie!" His words hurt me.

"I don't know, Maya. I thought you'd never sneak out of the house, but you did. I never thought you'd date another guy, but you have. It's hard for me to believe that you did *not* go all the way with him," Misalo said as he began backing away from me.

"And what about you and Viviana? What does dating my cousin say about you as a person?" I fired back at him.

"So it is true. You did go all the way with him." Misalo seemed transfixed on how far I'd gone with Carlo.

"Why do you even care? You were so busy running behind Viviana like she was the best thing that ever happened to you. How did you feel when you found out how she had played you for a fool?" I bluntly asked. My question left Misalo speechless and his ego bruised.

"I've got to go," Misalo said and swam away to the other end of the swimming pool. He got out of the water, dried himself off and then left. I tried to hold on to my tears, but it was of no use. I buried my face in my hands and cried. I wanted Misalo back. I wanted the love we had to restore itself, but I didn't know if we could forgive each other.

four

I had just finished styling my hair and covering up my bruised skin with makeup. I put on a pair of sexy blue jeans and a nice top. I wanted to look as decent as I could because I had to speak to Misalo. I needed him to understand that everything I did and said regarding Maya was fully justified. After he heard what I had to say, I was certain he'd forgive me, and we could continue dating.

Once my hair and makeup were flawless, I called Misalo. I didn't get an answer, but that did not stop me from calling him several times. After calling him at least ten times without an answer, I decided I'd go to his house and beg for five minutes of his time. As I walked out of the house, I saw Maya, who had just returned from the swimming pool. She looked as if she'd been crying, but I didn't really care about her emotional state. I only cared about reclaiming Misalo before she tried to sink her hooks into him.

"Slut!" Maya spat the word at me as she walked past me. I flipped up my middle finger as I moved on out the door. While I walked toward Misalo's house, I called him again, but still got no answer. As luck would have it, I caught up with him as he was exiting a local pizzeria.

"Misalo," I called out his name as I quickened my pace

to catch up to him. When he turned in the direction of my voice, his facial expression turned sour.

"What do you want, Viviana?" he asked disdainfully.

"I know you're mad at me, and you have every right to be," I began speaking at a fast pace.

"I don't have anything to say to you." Misalo turned his back to me and started walking toward his car.

"Please just give me five minutes to explain," I begged him.

"Explain what, Viviana? You're a sneaky liar, and I don't like being around people like you. End of story." Misalo's words stabbed my heart.

"I deserved that and you're right. I was sneaky and I stretched the truth in order to get back at Maya, but aren't you curious as to why?" I asked, hoping he would be interested in understanding my justification.

"No." Misalo opened his car door. I hustled over to the passenger door and pulled the handle. Thankfully the door was unlocked and I got in the car with him.

"What the hell, Viviana. Get out!" Misalo shouted at me. I didn't move. I sat in the car with my head slumped submissively between my shoulders. I felt horrible about how I'd misled him, but I didn't want him to hate me for it.

"Get out of my car, Viviana," he yelled at me again. I looked at him and sniffled. Misalo met my gaze only for a moment and then turned away. "I'm not hearing it, girl. Get out before I come over and yank you out of the car seat."

"Please, Misalo. Just let me get this off my chest." My voice trembled and I smeared away the tears that were trickling down my cheeks.

"Viviana, get out of my car!" Misalo clenched his teeth

as he spoke. I sat still and refused to move. I was going to make him hear me out one way or the other.

"Listen to what I have to say and then I'll get out," I promised.

"Talk." Misalo released a deep sigh and finally gave in.

"Maya and I have been enemies for a long time. Because of her, my father is dead and I hate her for it. Because of her, my life was ruined. Being forced to live with her is the hardest thing ever."

"So you used me to get back at her. I got it. Now get out," Misalo said.

"No, it's not like that. I mean—" I paused and tried to determine if I should be 100 percent truthful or continue to lie "—yes. At first, I only wanted to break up your relationship because I had gotten so sick and tired of hearing her brag about how perfect you were."

"Wow, with a cousin like you, who needs enemies?" Misalo's words stabbed me deeply.

"I'm not an evil person, Misalo. I only tempted you by showing you a different way of looking at your relationship with Maya. That's all. If you trusted her fully and were truly in love with her, nothing I said should have mattered."

"You manipulated me," Misalo said.

"No, I didn't. I fell in love with you. I did everything I could to protect that love and prove it to you," I explained. Misalo glanced over at me, and for a brief moment, I lost myself in his eyes.

"I developed real feelings for you. You're the first guy I've ever dated who seemed to really care about me. You actually talked to me and not at me. Whenever I would think about you, I would smile. I didn't anticipate developing true feelings."

"News flash, Viviana. You played me for a complete idiot. If that's your idea of affection, you can keep it." Misalo let me have it.

I placed my hand on his thigh and said, "If you would give me one more chance, I will show you how serious I am about you." Misalo's head craned downward and looked at where my hand was positioned on his thigh.

"Yes. That's what I mean. I am willing to prove how much I care for you. I want to give myself to you," I said earnestly. I wanted to be intimate with Misalo in every possible way. I didn't want him to deny my offer of reconciliation.

five

MAYA

"I can't believe today is my last day of work," Keysha said. It was Sunday at 10:30 a.m., and we were sitting next to each other on lawn chairs. We both had beach towels wrapped around our legs because the air had turned noticeably cooler.

"Well, I can't wait until next summer because I'm definitely going to be working here," I said, recalling how I enjoyed the excitement of being a lifeguard.

"I don't think anyone will be coming to the pool today," Keysha said, reaching into her bag for a book.

"Dang, girl! What are you reading now?" I asked sarcastically.

"Well, I have become pretty good friends with one of the librarians named Robbie. She knows how much I enjoy reading and makes some really good recommendations. I'm reading a Kimani TRU book."

"Is it any good?" I asked.

"I haven't started yet," Keysha answered as I fumbled with my cell phone. I opened up my Facebook app and updated my status. I let everyone know that I was chilling at the pool with my girl. I then clicked on to Misalo's Facebook page to read what his latest status update was.

"Oh, this is interesting," I said aloud.

"What?" Keysha asked as she shifted on her seat.

"Misalo says that he's going to an end-of-summer party," I said.

"Really? Who is throwing a party? I haven't heard anything about a party," Keysha said.

"Hang on. I'm still reading the details. It's an end-of-summer party and OMG." I stopped reading.

"What?" Keysha asked.

"Jerry is throwing the party," I said.

"What!" Keysha sat upright and moved closer to me so that she could see what was on my phone.

"See, it says Jerry is throwing the party." I showed Keysha.

"Well, I'm not going to that," Keysha said.

"Have you heard from him at all?" I asked, even though I already knew the answer.

"No, and I hope I never do." Keysha's attitude was clear. I knew for a fact that she didn't like Jerry at all.

"So let me get this straight. You were telling me that I should have forgiven Viviana when she called me up and asked for help when she was getting a beat down, but it sounds like you haven't forgiven Jerry at all."

"That's different," Keysha said.

"How?" I asked, giving her a chance to explain.

"Jerry and I could have had something really special, but he was too much of a jerk to realize it. But that's water under an old bridge now. Anyway, considering all the drama that took place at his last party, I'm surprised he has the guts to throw another one," Keysha said.

"Wait, wait, wait. Go back to the part where you said

you and Jerry could've had something special. Would you date him again?"

"Oh, God, no! Dating him was one of the biggest mistakes of my life," Keysha said as she repositioned herself and opened her book.

I turned my attention back to my phone and noticed that Viviana had posted a comment on Misalo's wall.

"What the hell!" I blurted out.

"What?" Keysha looked at me, startled.

"Viviana just posted something stupid on Misalo's wall," I said as I read her post again.

"What did she say?" Keysha leaned toward me.

"She said, 'I'll be there, too, baby. I can't wait to see you.'"

"Is Misalo still seeing her after the stunt she pulled on him?" I glanced at Keysha.

"I don't think so. I hope he's not that damn dumb," I said as I began typing with my thumbs.

"What are you posting?" Keysha asked.

"A nasty message to Viviana that says, 'I know you're not online flirting with my boyfriend, Viviana!'"

"Ooo! You're just going to call her out like that?" Keysha asked.

"Yeah, I want the world to know what type of tramp she is," I said, feeling rather evil. A few seconds later my phone buzzed, indicating that a response had been posted. I checked my phone and read the response from Viviana out loud.

@Maya. Yes I will be there with my man, and if you try to holla at him again, you're going to have to deal with me.

@Viviana. Find your own boyfriend! Misalo is taken, slut!

@Maya. You're the slut with the nasty pictures. Obviously he didn't like what he saw because he has been with me.

"Oh, that was a low blow," said Keysha, who was looking over my shoulder and reading the messages with me.

@Viviana. After you lied!

@Maya. Get over it!

@Viviana. I don't think so! You need to watch your back!

I posted and then shut off my phone.

"Dang, I am starting to think that Viviana might have some serious mental issues," said Keysha as she rubbed the tension from my shoulders.

"She's crazy, Keysha. That's what I've been trying to explain to you," I said as I combed my fingers through my hair.

"I see what you're saying," Keysha said.

"Keysha, I'm going to that party, and I want you to come with me," I said.

"Oh, no. I don't want to run into Jerry," Keysha said.

"You probably won't even see him. There should be tons of people there anyway," I said.

"Why do you want to go?" Keysha asked.

"Because I want to confront Misalo," I said.

"You've already done that."

"I'm not done with him yet," I said.

"Then call him and meet him somewhere," Keysha suggested.

"No. I want to surprise him. I want to catch him completely off guard and force him to give me real answers." Keysha and I looked at each other for a long moment without saying a word. She finally broke the silence.

"How long do you think it will take?" she asked.

"I don't know. It shouldn't take too long. Come on, Keysha, I really need your support," I begged.

"Fine! I'll go," Keysha reluctantly agreed.

The party at Jerry's house was massive. Kids parked their cars in the middle of the street because there were no more parking spaces. Since the party was in the middle of a weekday and had begun at 1:00 p.m., none of Jerry's neighbors were home to complain. Keysha and I followed the throngs of kids racing down the sidewalk toward the sound of loud music and squealing voices. Once we were inside, unfortunately the first person we ran into was Jerry, Keysha's old boyfriend. He was wearing a white T-shirt and blue shorts. His eyes were bloodshot, and I was sure it was from drinking, smoking or something else.

"Keysha." He smiled and stepped toward her for a hug. Keysha moved out of his way.

"Oh, it's like that?" Jerry asked disappointed.

"Yeah, it's like that," Keysha said.

"Come on. Don't tell me you're still mad at me?" Jerry whined.

"Jerry, what you did to me was awful." Keysha raised her voice.

"Give me a break. You're overreacting, Keysha. Besides,

that happened so long ago. You shouldn't hold grudges. I haven't held any against you." Jerry smiled again.

"I don't have time for this. Maya, let's find Misalo and then get out of here," Keysha said, moving away from Jerry.

"Hey, Keysha," he called out to her as we continued on. Keysha and I turned back to look at him.

"What?" Keysha asked, annoyed.

"Get out of my house!" Jerry said.

"What?" Keysha repeated, insulted.

"You heard me. Get the hell out of my house. Remember, this is my party. Not yours. Now get out," Jerry said more forcefully.

"Jerry, give me a break, okay," I said, stepping toward him. "Keysha didn't want to come. I begged her to walk over with me. We're just here to find Misalo, and then we'll leave."

"You can stay, Maya. But Keysha. No way. She has to go." Jerry stood his ground.

"Jerry, you're such an ass. I don't know what I ever saw in you," Keysha said as she walked back past Jerry. I followed her out onto the sidewalk.

"Keysha, slow down," I said.

"Ooh! I'm so ticked off with him! Maya, I told you that I didn't want to come to this stupid party," Keysha griped as she marched down the street.

"I know and I'm sorry. I had no idea Jerry would react like that," I apologized.

"I'm not going back in there," she said.

"You don't have to. I'll go and find Misalo myself."

"Fine," Keysha said. She gave me a brief hug and then continued on. I turned around and headed back, determined to find Misalo.

SIX

VIVIANA

I really enjoyed ticking Maya off on Facebook. She had no idea that I had agreed to prove to Misalo that I was indeed the girl for him. When I arrived at the party, Misalo was sitting with some of his soccer friends. I walked over to where he was and sweetly asked one of his friends to move out of the seat next to him. Misalo looked surprised to see me. I leaned over, in front of all his friends, and purposely spoke in his ear.

"I know that you're not going to make me beg you," I whispered. Misalo looked at me as if he didn't trust me.

"Damn, I wish my girl would greet me like that!" I heard one of his guy friends say.

"You're not serious," Misalo said as he looked into my eyes.

"Yes, I am," I whispered in his ear again and nibbled on his earlobe.

"Maybe you guys need to get a hotel room," said another one of his friends jokingly.

"Don't want to wait any longer," I continued to speak in his ear. Then I reached over and kissed him. Just a quick one at first, then our lips met again for a longer kiss. I squeezed his thigh and rubbed his chest.

Pulling away I said, "I'm ready and I'm yours, Misalo, if you want me."

"Misalo, dude, if you don't take care of her needs, I will!" said yet another one of his friends.

I pressed my forehead against his, but Misalo didn't say anything.

"Please say something. I'm spilling my heart out to you," I pleaded.

"So if I said let's go do it right now, you'd go all the way?" asked Misalo.

"Yes. I'm serious about how much I love you," I said humbly. After that statement, he was all mine. We got up and walked out.

I got into his car, which was parked around the corner from Jerry's house. After a few moments, Misalo looked at me and said, "I know a place that we can go."

"Okay," I answered as he pulled off. We had to drive back past Jerry's house in order to get there. As he sped down the street, I noticed Maya and Keysha standing around. Keysha appeared to be very upset about something, but I didn't care. Misalo had not noticed them, and I certainly wasn't about to tell him that Maya was nearby. I didn't say a word. I snuggled up to his right arm and held on to it as he continued on.

Twenty minutes later, Misalo parked his car in front of a construction site where new homes were being built.

He popped the trunk and said, "Come on."

I got out of the car and waited as he grabbed a blanket from the trunk.

"Where are we going?" I finally spoke.

"Over there in one of the houses that they haven't put doors on yet. No will see us," he assured me.

"It's surrounded by a wooden fence that is too tall to climb over," I pointed out.

"Someone kicked out a few of the plywood planks toward the other end of the fence. The hole is covered by bushes, and I know that the construction workers haven't fixed it yet," Misalo said as he grabbed my hand and pulled me along. I suddenly got nervous and wanted him to be gentle and take his time with me.

"Will this be special?" I asked.

"What do you mean?" Misalo glanced back at me.

"Will you like me again once I do this?" I asked.

"Sure," Misalo said. We reached the opening in the fence and wiggled our way through it. We walked around the construction site, which was eerily silent. There were lots of concrete foundations that lacked framing and others that had the framework, but had not been enclosed with plywood and siding. At the rear of the construction site there was a home that was nearly complete. The doors were on it, but no locks had been installed.

"Are you sure we'll be safe in here?" I nervously asked.

"Yes," he said as I followed him inside. No drywall had been installed yet, but the rooms had been framed out with wood.

"We can do it right here." Misalo spread the blanket out over the floor, which was covered with sawdust.

"This isn't exactly what I had in mind," I mumbled as I hugged myself and rubbed my arms.

"It will be fine," Misalo whispered as he patted a spot for me to sit down on. I sat on the floor, which was hard and uncomfortable. He sat next to me.

"Do you have protection?" I asked, hoping that he was prepared.

"Yeah, I have something," he said as he proudly removed a condom. I swallowed hard and my lips quivered because I had no clue as to what to do next.

"So have you done it before?" I asked, not sure if it was the appropriate time to ask such a question.

"Have you?" he countered with a question of his own, which didn't make me feel comfortable. In my mind I always imagined that my first time would be with a more experienced guy.

"No," I whispered, hoping that my inexperience wouldn't ruin the moment.

"Neither have I, so we're both about to lose our virginity together." Misalo said it as if being a virgin was like being diseased. I was all for proving my love, but I needed to know that his love for me was just as strong.

"So what's next?" I asked, too afraid to ask the love question out of fear I'd be rejected.

"We do it," he said as he began to unlatch his belt buckle.

"Wait." I stopped him. "Kiss me first, please," I begged.

"Okay," Misalo answered as he mounted himself on top of me.

I thought kissing would turn me on and get me in a better mood and even perhaps make me forget about how uncomfortable the floor felt. Misalo kissed me clumsily as if he couldn't have cared less about kissing me the right way. He paused for a moment and glanced down at me. I saw a strange expression on his face, but I wasn't sure what the look meant. He kissed me roughly again.

"Softer," I whispered instructions. "Kiss me softer." He began placing softer kisses on my neck and thrust his hips into me. My hands trembled as I locked my arms around his back and held him close.

"Do you love me?" I spoke purposefully in his ear.

"Yes, Maya, I do," he answered. His breath on my skin suddenly felt like a hot blowtorch.

"What!" I shoved him off me so quickly he probably thought I saw someone spying on us.

"What's wrong?" he asked, confused.

"You called me Maya!" I said, feeling like smoke from a candle that had just been snuffed out.

"I did?" He paused and replayed in his mind what he'd said. "It was a mistake. Relax." He tried to make me feel as if I were overreacting.

"How could you think about her at a time like this?" I immediately stood up. I felt unimportant, as if the feelings I had were not mutual.

"It was a slip of the tongue. I didn't mean anything by it," he said defensively. "Come on, don't ruin the moment."

"Me, ruin the moment? Huh! You've done that on your own. I can't believe you!" I said as I began walking away.

"Where are you going?" he asked, suddenly realizing just how serious saying the wrong name was.

"You totally killed the mood I was in. You've messed up everything, Misalo. I'm nothing like Maya. You, of all people, should know that," I said, feeling blinding rage growing inside me. I needed to get away and calm down because, at that moment, I could have easily taken the claw end of a hammer and struck him with it.

Once I got outside the construction area, I began running. I wanted to escape from everything—Misalo, my family and, if I could, my life. Once I was a good distance away, I sat down on a bus stop bench and sobbed. Misalo truly did care about Maya more than me. The fact that I was about to endear myself to him meant nothing. As I sat on the bench, I realized that I was an emotional train wreck. My emotions functioned like a roller coaster ride—when my feelings took a nosedive, my stomach always ended up in my throat. The only constant feeling in my life was my hatred for Maya.

"Viviana." Misalo found me. I looked over my shoulder and glanced at him briefly as he walked toward me. I smeared away my tears and pushed my emotions deep down inside.

"What?" I snarled at him, like a wounded animal giving a final warning before attacking.

"I'm sorry. I don't know what else to say."

I glanced at him. He looked pathetic, like some chubby nerd attempting to ask a cheerleader to the school dance.

"Take me home," I said abruptly. He'd ticked me off to the point that the very sight of him was upsetting.

seven

MAYA

"YOU will not believe what Misalo has done," I complained to Keysha as we entered the beauty salon. We had both made appointments. Keysha was getting her hair braided again, and I was getting a manicure and pedicure. We sat in the waiting area because the salon was packed and filled with the sounds of multiple conversations taking place all at once. I recognized a few girls from school and waved to them. I assumed they were there for the same reasons Keysha and I were. School. Classes would be starting soon, and any girl who had any kind of sense knew that she had better come to school on the first day looking like a magazine cover model.

"Nothing surprises me anymore when it comes to Misalo," Keysha admitted as she searched the table in front of us for a magazine.

"He slept with Viviana." I leaned toward Keysha and whispered so no one else could hear what I had to say. The words left a bitter taste on my tongue.

"What!" Keysha blurted out as if some teacher had just handed her a test paper with a fat red F on it. Several people looked in our direction to see what the commotion was about. Some of them had a look in their eyes that suggested they were anticipating a cat fight between me and Keysha. Keysha realized that she had spoken louder than she intended so she leaned in closer and whispered.

"They went all the way?" she asked for clarification.

"Yes," I answered with certainty.

"How do you know?" Keysha glanced at me suspiciously, wondering how I would find out such a thing.

"Viviana admitted it," I answered with a disgusted sigh.

"Maya, you and I both know you can't believe a thing Viviana says. She's a liar," Keysha reminded me.

"I know, but for some reason I believe she told the truth. When she came in the house yesterday, she had this strange look on her face. I wanted to ask her what was wrong, but decided not to. I was too busy trying to figure out why Misalo wasn't at the big party. I had searched all over Jerry's house looking for Misalo, but did not find him. And his so-called friends were of no help. They claimed they had not seen him, but I knew they were lying. Anyway, the last thing I wanted her to think was that I cared. Then Viviana went downstairs to talk to Anna. I don't know why, but something made me walk halfway down the steps and stand out of their eyesight to eavesdrop on their conversation. I clearly heard Viviana say that she and Misalo decided to go all the way."

"Wow," Keysha said as she came to realize how serious I was.

"What did you do then?" she asked.

"Nothing. I walked back up the stairs, disgusted and ticked off with Misalo and Viviana."

"So what does that mean? Are you finally done with him?" Keysha asked.

"That's like me asking you if you're finally done with Wesley," I said condescendingly.

Keysha raised her eyebrow at me.

"I'm sorry," I apologized. "I have no idea what my next move will be."

"Perhaps it's time to let it go," Keysha suggested.

"That's not the advice I want to hear," I unashamedly admitted.

"You can't make Misalo want you, Maya. If he is not making an effort to patch things up, then there is really nothing more you can do," Keysha said.

"Yeah. I know," I said, feeling rather depressed about it. Never in a million years would I have ever thought that Misalo would give himself so freely to another girl. What's even more insulting and disrespectful is that he had sex with my cousin. Although I was very disappointed with Misalo, I still cared about him. I couldn't turn my feelings for him off like a light switch on a wall.

I'd just taken a seat at the pedicure station which was situated near the front window. I briefly glanced at the black letters which spelled out the name of the salon. Just as I'd submerged my feet into a footbath filled with warm water, someone knocked hard on the glass. I turned in the direction of the sound and saw Carlo waving at me.

"Oh, great," I mumbled. "He's the last person I want to see." I smiled at him out of politeness and hoped he would move on. Unfortunately, I wasn't that lucky.

Carlo opened the door to the salon and a bell chimed.

"What's up, girl?" He smiled at me. He had on a blue-and-white-striped polo shirt, blue jeans and a pair of black

Air Force 1 gym shoes. He also had sunglasses resting on top of his head.

"Same old stuff," I answered as I looked down at my feet and wiggled my toes. I had not seen Carlo since he had the fight with Misalo.

"Where have you been?" Carlo asked.

"Around." I gave him a vague answer.

"Around where?" Carlo wanted me to share more than I was willing to offer.

"Why do you even care?" I said with an irritated tone that I had hoped would force him to turn around and leave. As far as I was concerned, I never wanted to see him again. It was over between us, and I didn't want to go our separate ways on friendly terms.

"That's a good question. I don't know why I care about you, especially since you have a nasty attitude."

"You helped to create my attitude toward you." I hoped my words felt like a red-hot knife piercing his skin.

"You know, Maya, you're a real..."

"Hey, don't you dare say what I think you're about to say," said Kim, the shop owner, who was nearby.

"You're a real pain, Maya," Carlo said.

I ignored him. I couldn't believe he had come into the salon just to insult me.

"I'm so glad it's over between us, Carlo," I said, waving for him to go away and bother someone else.

"One of these days, Maya, someone is going to put your prissy attitude in check. I tried to be a good guy for you. A guy who didn't play games, a guy who tried to be real with you. Instead, you put me down for some jerk who cheated on you. You talk about how you're glad it's over. Hell, I'm the one who is glad it's over." Carlo gave me a nasty look before turning to walk out.

eight

VIVIANA

I had told Anna all about how Misalo ruined everything by calling out Maya's name. Misalo had humiliated and hurt me in a way that I never thought possible. There had been days when I really felt bad, but that incident with him took the cake. Anna listened and was sympathetic, but beyond that there was nothing that could be done. It was over between Misalo and me, and that hurt me more than I ever thought it would. I truly liked him. I appreciated his honesty. Even though I had twisted the truth to get his attention, it was, in my opinion, well worth the lies I'd told. He gave me the type of attention I longed for, but now that was gone and the hole in my heart was as big as a crater on the surface of the moon.

The following morning I saw Maya in the upstairs hallway. She was heading downstairs, and I was on my way to the bathroom.

"Slut!" Maya said as she walked past me.

"What did you just say to me?" I asked.

"Our truce is over. I don't like you. I don't want you in my house, and I'm going to make sure that I do everything that I can to get you kicked out." Maya's eyes were ablaze with an evilness that I'd never seen before. I didn't feel like getting into a battle of words with her so I just flipped up my middle finger and continued on.

When I came downstairs, I ran into my aunt Raven, who was carrying a basket of laundry.

"Come with me, Viviana," she said.

"Why? What's up?" I asked, wondering if I'd done something wrong.

"I want to talk to you," said Aunt Raven. I exhaled and followed her to her bedroom where she began folding her laundry.

"I've contacted your school and had your records transferred over to Thornwood," she began.

"Okay," I said, dreading the fact that I'd have to repeat my junior year of high school.

"You're going to have to be tested. Your entire junior year is filled with incomplete grades."

"I told you why," I said defensively.

"I know your mom kept moving you around," Aunt Raven said.

"I hate tests. Why can't they just let me come in as a senior?" I grumbled at the idea of having to deal with some stupid multiple-choice exam where I had to use a No. 2 black pencil to fill in a circle.

"Honey, schools use standardized tests to determine if you have a learning disability or some other handicap," Aunt Raven said as she moved to a nearby closet and removed several hangers.

"I'm not stupid," I said with an edge in my voice.

"I know that," Aunt Raven said.

"Then why didn't you tell them?" I was getting emotional, but couldn't help it.

"Watch your tone with me," Aunt Raven warned. "You'll

be tested on basic stuff. Reading Comprehension, English, Math and Science. It's a way for the school to find out what courses they should place you in."

"I still think tests are stupid," I said, loathing the idea.

"You take the test first thing tomorrow morning," she said.

"Are you serious? They won't even give me time to study?"

"I'm afraid not," said Aunt Raven.

"Augh, that sucks," I complained as I plopped down on the bed.

"Don't worry about it. Just go in there and do the best that you can," she said. I cut my eyes at her as if I were about to stab her.

"I have a question for you," she said.

"What?" I mumbled a little as I felt a small anxiety attack swelling up.

"When was the last time you had a physical?" she asked.

"I don't know. Mom rarely took me to the doctor. She doesn't have health insurance," I said.

"Okay. Do you remember the name of the last doctor you saw?" she asked.

"I have no idea. The only thing I remember was that she was Korean, and she was still learning how to be a doctor."

"What do you mean, she was still learning how to be a doctor?"

My answer seemed to have alarmed her. "She was in training. Down at Cook County Hospital," I said.

"Oh, you mean she was doing a residency," said Aunt Raven.

"Yeah, whatever that is," I answered. Aunt Raven paused

for a moment and then said, "I'm going to call your grandmother and see if she has any of your medical records."

"What for? I'm not sick," I said.

"School, dear. Anna, Paul, Maya and you need to get a
physical for school, and I have to get as much of your medical history together as possible."

"Oh," I said, then turned my thoughts to Maya and how
she had threatened me earlier.

"I've scheduled an appointment for later this week."

"Fine," I said. "Is that it?"

"That will do it," she said, trying to sound upbeat and as
if I wasn't an additional burden on her. I don't know why,
but I felt lousy. I felt as if I didn't belong here and that I was
more trouble than I was worth.

I walked back to the kitchen to get myself something to
snack on. Shortly thereafter Paul walked into the kitchen
with his skateboard that had graffiti-styled lettering that
read Fly Higher. Paul quickly made himself a peanut but-
ter and jelly sandwich and sat down at the table to eat it.

"What's up?" he asked as he bit into his sandwich then
removed a handheld game from his pocket.

"Nothing." I released a long uncomfortable sigh. I opened
the refrigerator door and was moving a few things around
to see if there was any more Jell-O left when I heard Maya
ask, "What are you doing in our refrigerator?" Startled, I
popped my head up and looked at her. She was standing
on the other side of the door glaring at me. The evil in her
eyes was unmistakable.

"Excuse me," I said, as if her comment was meaningless.

"If you're going to eat our food, you need to ask first,"
Maya said, making up her own rules.

"No, I don't," I snapped at her and shut the refrigerator

door so that it was no longer between us. Maya lowered her eyelids to slits. She clenched her teeth and for the very first time, I saw just how much she truly despised me.

"Do you hate me?" I asked with a sly smile. I knew I was pushing her buttons of contempt for me.

"Yes," she answered without hesitation.

"Now you know exactly how cold my heart is toward you," I said and waited for her to throw a punch or reach for my hair. I was ready for her, but in true Maya fashion, she chickened out. She turned her back to me and stormed away like a spoiled brat.

The following morning I walked up to Thornwood High School to take the standardized test. Once inside, a security guard pointed in the direction of the library, which is where I was supposed to go. When I arrived, I was asked to sign in by a woman standing behind a counter. I assumed she was one of the teachers here. After I signed in, she looked down at my name. "Hello, Viviana," said the woman. She had an even brown complexion and a warm, pretty smile.

"Hi," I said as I began glancing around.

"You can have a seat anywhere. There are a few more kids coming in," she informed me. I exhaled out of frustration before stepping away to sit on one of the hard wooden chairs. Several other kids wandered in and sat down at other tables that were nearby. Then I heard this loud voice. I turned in the direction of it, and, through the glass, I saw this girl talking loudly to the security guard.

"This is the library, right?" she asked, pointing.

"Duh," I whispered to myself. All she had to do was look at all the books to figure out that this was the library. She walked through the entrance.

"What's up? Are you the librarian in this joint?" She was talking as if there was loud music playing and no one could hear her.

"Shhh, yes," said the teacher as she pointed to the sign-in sheet. The girl picked up the ink pen and signed in.

"Shhh, back to you. I'm not even registered yet," said the girl as she slammed the pen down on the countertop.

"Take a seat," said the teacher.

"Anywhere?" she asked.

"Yes."

"Please don't sit next to me," I whispered to myself as I looked in another direction, pretending to be interested in the READ posters on the wall.

"Yo. Is this spot taken?"

I turned my attention toward her. She was pointing to the seat that was on the opposite side of my table. "No," I answered.

"Cool. I'm going to park it right here," she said as she sat down and began tapping the pads of her fingertips on the edge of the table. She began humming the lyrics to a popular song.

"Where are you from?" she asked.

"Around," I answered.

"I can tell that because you don't look like you're from around here."

I didn't know if I should be insulted or take what she said as a compliment.

"Are you from Chicago or someplace else? Because you are damn sure not from these lame-ass suburbs," she said, looking directly into my eyes.

"How do you know that?" I asked curiously.

"I've been around and can tell things about people right

away. For example, I know you're not a suburban girl because you just don't have the look. You don't look like the type who goes out horseback riding, so I know you're not a country girl," she said as she continued to thump her fingers against the table while nodding to some rhythm that was playing in her head.

"City girl," I answered.

"You mean hood chick." She chuckled.

"Yeah, something like that," I said, glaring at her. I was trying to figure her out.

"That's cool, because I'm definitely hood. My name is LaShaunda Hackett." She curled her fist and offered up a fist bump. I gave her one.

"Viviana," I answered. LaShaunda was a lighter shade of brown. Her black hair had light brown highlights and was pulled back away from her face. Her hairline had been overprocessed and as a result, the amount of hair around the rim of her face was sparse. She had thick black eyebrows that needed to be trimmed and her name was tattooed on her neck. I glanced down at her hands and noticed that several of her knuckles had dark black scabs that had formed to heal a wound. I immediately knew that she was a fighter. LaShaunda was overweight, but thankfully, she wasn't the type of chick who wore clothes that were too small.

"I like that name. It's kind of sexy," she said and I laughed.

"No one has ever said that before," I remarked, feeling myself letting my guard down a little. "Who did you get into a fight with?" I asked. LaShaunda slapped her hand down on the table.

"I knew you were hood. Only a hood chick would know that busted knuckles come from fighting. The moment I saw you, I knew we'd get along."

I laughed fretfully. LaShaunda had a personality that was large, loud and very bold.

"I got into a situation where I had to protect myself. You know what I'm saying?" she asked.

"Yeah, I know what you're saying," I answered.

"You see, I'm from Milwaukee. Where I come from, we handle our business. Nobody messed with our crew. We did it all, girl, and I can't wait to get back there."

"Wait, what are you doing here if you're from Milwaukee?" I asked.

LaShaunda leaned back on the legs of the chair, curled her lips into a sour expression and said, "Some BS."

"Shhh," the teacher warned LaShaunda again.

"What the hell do I have to be quiet for?" LaShaunda turned and asked the teacher, who seemed stunned by LaShaunda's explosive reaction. When the teacher didn't answer, LaShaunda turned her attention back to me.

"School hasn't even started and she's already on a power trip," LaShaunda griped.

"Like I was saying, my crew, we're like family, we look out for each other," she continued to explain.

"It would be nice to have a family like that," I said, feeling the sting of being a burden to my aunt Raven and being loathed by Maya.

"So what are you in here for?" LaShaunda asked.

"Some stupid placement test," I answered.

"Yeah, me, too. I told these mo fos that I'm not stupid, and that I have more sense in my farts than they have in their head." I laughed so hard that I grunted like a pig.

"You don't believe me? I can cut one right now to prove it," LaShaunda said.

"No, please don't," I said as I smeared away a few tears

of laughter. "If I laugh any harder, I'll end up peeing on myself."

"You seem like a pretty cool chick," LaShaunda said. "You don't seem all fake and phony. I like that."

"I always keep it real," I said.

LaShaunda leaned closer to me and whispered, even though her version of a whisper was still loud. "You ever do anything illegal?" she asked.

"I'm no angel," I answered. "Why?"

"After this test, I'm heading downtown to the Lollapalooza Music Fest. If you're not afraid to jump a fence, then we could spend the rest of the day having the time of our lives."

"Oh, man, I've always wanted to go to Lollapalooza." LaShaunda smiled at me. "Then it sounds to me like we've got a plan."

"How are we going to get downtown?" I asked.

"Just stick with me, girl. I'll get us there," LaShaunda said.

Then out of nowhere, a wicked idea popped into my head. "Hey, do you like making some fast money?" I asked.

"Does a bear take a dump in the woods?" LaShaunda answered my question with another one.

"I have to stop by my house and pick up something before we go," I said.

"What do you need to get?" she asked.

"A backpack," I answered.

"Girl, why do you want to carry a backpack around?" LaShaunda asked.

"Do you want to make some money or ask questions?"

"All right." LaShaunda smiled and pointed her finger at me. "I'm down with whatever you have planned. Money always makes me smile," she said.

nine

MAYA

I called Keysha to see if she wanted to hang out and got the shock of my life when she said she and Wesley were going out.

"Huh?" I said as I pulled my cell phone away from my ear and glared at it. I was certain that I didn't hear what Keysha had said correctly.

"I know. I said I didn't think I'd ever go out with him again, but I decided to give him another chance." It was hard to tell if Keysha was trying to convince me or herself that giving Wesley another chance was worth the effort.

"After all the heartache you went through with him, what could he have possibly said to make you want to give him another chance?" I asked.

"He and I have been talking more lately, and we've gotten to be friends again, but we're going to take our relationship slow this time," Keysha explained.

"Oh, give me a break," I griped as I stuck my finger in my mouth and pretended to vomit.

"I told him that if I see him doing anything remotely close to drinking alcohol or otherwise, that was it. I would not allow him to make a fool of me again."

"Where are you guys going?" I asked with a sarcastic sigh.

"He has tickets to the Lollapalooza Music Festival. Do you want to come with us?" Keysha asked.

"No, I don't want to be the third wheel," I said, trying to conceal my envy.

"I know this is going to sound totally crazy, but maybe you could come down with your sister or brother."

"No one is home. I am here all alone." I hoped I would get a sympathetic reaction.

"Are you sure you don't want me to have Wesley pick you up?" Keysha offered again.

I exhaled. "No. You guys go on and have a good time. I'll be fine. Call me when you get back," I said.

"Okay," Keysha solemnly said and then ended the call. A few moments later I received a text from her.

R U really, really sure u don't want 2 go?

Yes. TTYL

My mom and dad had left to attend one of Anna's modeling competitions and my brother was out, probably getting into mischief with his friends. Viviana was at Thornwood High School taking a placement test. I told myself that she'd probably do so horribly that she would end up in remedial classes. The thought made me smile because I knew academically I would run circles around her. The thought of Viviana made me feel evil. I wanted her out of my house and I secretly wished there was a way I could make my parents see that she was nothing but bad news. Then they would be forced to ship her back to Grandmother Esmeralda.

I grabbed my laptop computer and headed down to the family room. I decided to log on to my Tumblr account to

see what was going on while simultaneously watching TV.
Once I got settled comfortably on the sofa, I picked up the
remote and aimed it at the television. I turned it to VH1
Soul and then booted up my laptop. When my computer
screen came up, I noticed that my wallpaper image was a
photo of me and Misalo. The photo was taken a while ago,
but it was one of my favorites. It captured us kissing on a
carnival ride called the Sizzler. The only thing that was really sizzling was the kiss. I was about to delete the photo so
I'd stop thinking about him, but I didn't. Instead, I typed
in the URL for YouTube and pulled up a song by Beyoncé
called "I Miss You." I began singing along as I studied our
photo. My heart was so broken. Tears began forming in my
eyes and it wasn't long before my nose was running and I
was smearing away tears from my cheeks.

"I miss you, Misalo," I spoke aloud. I was so lost in
thought that I had not noticed that Viviana had walked into
the family room from the garage. She snickered at me. I
quickly scrambled to turn the music down and pretend that
I wasn't in that much emotional pain.

"What's up with her?" asked the big girl who was with
Viviana. She was as tall as a tree and she looked hardened.
She had not removed her shoes at the door as Viviana had
when she walked in. Everyone knew to remove their shoes
upon entering someone's home. It was common sense. I
immediately had a problem with Viviana's new friend. She
didn't have on any makeup, her hair was jacked up, and her
eyebrows were thick and bushy. She had on a sleeveless top
and I noticed she had dark skin blemishes on her arms. She
had on blue jeans and worn-out gym shoes. I cast judgment
on her, and concluded that wherever she had come from,
it wasn't too far from hell.

"She's the Antichrist," Viviana said as she and the girl walked past me.

"Mom and Dad don't like strangers in the house, Viviana. You can't have company," I said to her as they continued on.

"LaShaunda is not a stranger," Viviana said as she escorted the girl upstairs.

"You can't go upstairs," I said, as I got out of my chair and chased after them.

"Calm down, Paris Hilton. I am not going to rob the place." LaShaunda wrinkled her nose at me as if I smelled like rotting roadkill in the street.

"My name isn't Paris," I shot back, not liking the fact that she was comparing me to the snotty rich girl.

"Could've fooled me." LaShaunda cut her eyes at me.

"Maya, go sit in the basement and finish crying."

Viviana's words cut me deeply.

"What was she crying about?" asked LaShaunda as she continued to follow Viviana.

"Probably over her ex-boyfriend that I stole from her. I noticed she had a picture of them on her computer screen," Viviana said coolly.

"Damn! For real? You took her man?" LaShaunda asked.

"Yep."

"You're cold-blooded. I like that. You see something you want and you take it." LaShaunda continued to praise Viviana.

I stood at the bottom of the basement staircase that led up to the bedrooms feeling my earlier emotion of sorrow get replaced with hatred. I wanted Viviana to suffer. I wanted to make her feel miserable. Then, somewhere from a dark corner of my mind, I got a really wicked idea. I suddenly knew exactly how I was going to get back at Viviana and make her miserable at the same time.

I hustled upstairs and entered the kitchen. I saw Viviana's friend rifling through the refrigerator.

"What are you doing?" I asked angrily.

"Getting some food," she answered.

"Where is Viviana?" I asked.

"In the bathroom."

"So you just decided to raid our refrigerator?" I was appalled.

"Yeah, I was thirsty." She pulled out a can of soda and popped the top. The soda fizzled and liquid bubbled over, ran down the side of the can and her fingers and spilled onto the floor.

"Did Viviana tell you to go into our refrigerator?"

"Hell, no. I was thirsty so I decided to get me something to drink. Do you have a problem?"

"Yeah, you're rude," I said, wanting to snatch the can away from her. The girl answered by rolling her eyes at me.

"Who is going to clean up the spilled soda?" I pointed to the floor. She smirked, stepped to the wet spot on the floor and smeared the liquid farther with the bottom of her shoe.

When Viviana came out of the bathroom I told her what her friend had done.

"It's not a big deal, Maya. Just clean it up," Viviana said unapologetically. I was so furious that I wanted to throw something at Viviana's head.

They headed upstairs toward the bedrooms while I stared at the wet stain on the floor and allowed my heart to grow cold. A short time later they came downstairs with backpacks. Curiosity got the best of me.

"Where are you going with the backpacks?" I asked.

"Damn, Paris. Are you a spy or something?" LaShaunda was clearly irritated. I got a bad vibe from her.

"Remember, I told you that she's a snitch," Viviana said.

"That's right, you told me about what she did. She can't keep her mouth shut. If there is one type of person I can't stand, it's a snitch." LaShaunda glared at me in disgust. I had not known her five minutes, and she was behaving as if I was scum stuck to the bottom of her shoe.

"Excuse me," I raised my voice at LaShaunda.

"What's wrong, Paris? Are you feeling like a frog? Do you want to jump into a fight?" In addition to being ugly, LaShaunda was also a short-tempered bully.

"My name isn't Paris, it's Maya. And if you call me that again, I'm going to have to ask you to leave." I stood my ground even though I was nervous. Viviana seemed to get twisted joy out of the catfight LaShaunda and I were having.

"Come on, girl. You are wild." Viviana chuckled as she grabbed LaShaunda's arm and they walked away.

"That's okay," I said aloud. "You just wait."

I hustled back upstairs and walked down the hallway to Paul's room. The walls were blue, and the ceiling and wood trim baseboards were white. His bed was positioned directly in the center of the room, beneath the ceiling fan. On the far wall, in front of me, he had blown up several photos of himself doing aerial skateboarding acrobatics at a nearby skateboarding rink. On the right side of the room were several skateboards and a desk full of magazines, DVDs and a laptop computer. On the left side was his closet, which was unorganized and cluttered.

"What I'm looking for is probably in there," I mumbled to myself. Paul always kept gag gifts in his room that he

often used on his friends. On April Fools' Day I remembered that he had purchased itching powder, specifically to
try on one of his friends. All I needed to do was find out
where he had stashed the remainder of it.

Once I located the itching powder, I hustled down the
hallway to Anna's room. I located where Viviana kept her
underwear and sprinkled some of the powder in all of her
bras. I kept giggling to myself as I did it because she'd feel
compelled to scratch her breasts, but it would look so tacky
to do it in front of people. I couldn't wait for Viviana to return and get what was coming to her.

ten

VIVIANA

LaShaunda and I boarded a bus. She got on first and immediately took a seat. I paid my fare with a few bucks I'd managed to stash. I glanced at LaShaunda, wondering why she hadn't paid.

"Girl, I know you got me," she said as if I'd been informed in advance that I'd cover her expenses. I reluctantly paid her fare before going to sit near her.

"Thanks," she said.

I was silent. I was a little sore about the move she'd pulled.

"Don't worry," she said, sensing my agitation. "I'm going to give it back to you. I'm not like that. Just cover me for today. I'm good for it."

"Well, you should've said something before now." I cut my eyes at her.

"Okay, my bad. Just relax though. We're about to go and have a good time," she said, smiling at me. I knew that she was trying to change my sour mood.

"You owe me big-time," I said, finally letting go of my bitter disposition.

"Yeah, I know," she said solemnly. We arrived at the train station and I purchased tickets for us from a machine. We walked out onto the train platform and I curiously glanced down the track to see if the train was coming.

"Do you know how long we have to wait?" LaShaunda asked. I shrugged my shoulders.

"I don't know the schedule, but I think they run every hour." I pulled out my cell phone and looked at the time. It was 12:45 p.m.

"We shouldn't have to wait too long," I said. I walked farther down the platform and sat on the bench seat. LaShaunda joined me.

"So what's your story?" she asked.

"What do you mean?" I asked.

"I don't get you. I thought you were a hood chick, but you live in a large house with Paris Hilton who treats you like Cinderella. Are you a foster kid?" she asked.

I leaned forward and rested my forearms on my thighs. "Nope. She's my stuck-up cousin and I can't stand her," I said, feeling my blood heat.

"So why are you there?" LaShaunda asked.

"I was forced to live there. I was in a bad situation," I admitted.

Exhaling, LaShaunda said, "I know all about bad situations."

"Well, mine is pretty jacked up," I said.

"Couldn't be more jacked up than mine," LaShaunda said as she leaned her back against the bench and crossed her arms.

"I doubt it. My situation involves jail time and murder," I said, feeling certain LaShaunda's situation couldn't match the hell I'd gone through.

"Murder? Really?" LaShaunda leaned forward and rested her forearms on her thighs just like I had.

"Did you have to kill someone?" LaShaunda whispered as she looked around to make certain no one else had joined us on the platform.

"No," I said.

"Then what are you talking about?" LaShaunda laughed nervously.

"My father. They said he killed someone. He was sent to prison for it and was murdered while he was locked up," I explained.

"Who is 'they'? People trip me out when they say that. Is there a collection of people who stand around and say, I'm 'they' and I know about everything?" LaShaunda was being sarcastic.

"Well, in this instance, the 'they' would be my cousin, Maya, or Paris Hilton as you like to call her."

"Wait a minute. Are you saying that your cousin snitched on your father?"

LaShaunda was quick. "That's exactly what I'm saying."

"He went to jail for something he didn't do and was killed by someone?" LaShaunda asked.

"That's what I just told you. Why are you repeating it?" I said, feeling edgy. Whenever I think about Maya and my dad, I get angry.

"Dang, that is messed up. You're living in the house with a snitch. I can't stand people like that," LaShaunda said.

"Well, neither can I," I admitted.

"So how did you end up living with her?" LaShaunda was full of questions.

"My mother. She can't get a job and she walked out on me for a guy," I said, wondering why I was sharing all of my secrets with her.

"I understand. I know what that's like," LaShaunda said.

I stood up and glanced down the track again and saw the train approaching.

"The train is just about here," I informed LaShaunda. A few seconds later the train stopped and we boarded. Our car was almost empty so we sat in seats near the rear.

"Dang, my feet hurt," LaShaunda said as she slipped off her gym shoe. She took her foot out and wiggled her toes. It was then that I noticed that she didn't have any shoelaces.

"Why don't you have any shoelaces?" I asked.

"I can't believe you just asked me that question." LaShaunda glanced at me.

I remained silent, waiting for an answer.

"Okay, hood test," LaShaunda said.

"Hood test?" I was confused.

"Yeah. This is where I test your level of hood knowledge." She smirked.

"Okay," I said suspiciously.

"When your feet have outgrown your shoes, and you don't have money for a new pair, what do you do?" she asked.

"You remove the shoelaces so that you have a little more foot room," I said, immediately knowing the answer to the question.

"Correct. You've just answered your own question," LaShaunda said, slipping her foot back into the shoe. I suddenly felt dumb for asking my question. I, too, had done the same thing when my feet outgrew my shoes. In the summertime, when I lived with my mother, I just wore flip-flops so that I would not have to deal with the pain of scrunching my toes.

"So what's your story?" I asked.

"You don't want to hear about my screwed-up life,"

LaShaunda said. Her voice was suddenly distant as if the question caused her to go deep within herself.

"Hey, I've just spilled my guts out to you. The least you can do is do the same," I snapped at her.

She glanced at me. The look in her eyes was a murderous one, and I didn't exactly know what to make of it.

"You ever get high?" she asked.

"No," I said.

"I do," she admitted. "It keeps my nerves calm."

"That's not healthy," I stated, pointing out the obvious.

"I know. I can stop at any time. It's not like I'm addicted or something. I know that I can stop whenever I want to."

"I don't think you can smoke on the train," I said, believing that she wanted to smoke weed.

"I'm good. I only get high with I'm stressed out," she said.

"Stop avoiding my question, LaShaunda."

"Oh, yeah. That. What do you want to know?" LaShaunda scratched the side of her neck.

"What was your father like?" I asked.

"I met him once, when I was two. At least that is what my mother told me. I haven't seen or heard from him since," LaShaunda said.

"What about your mom? What is she like?" I asked.

"Psst. My mom is crazy. She doesn't like me and I don't like her," LaShaunda said.

"You sound like you're angry with her," I said.

"You could say that," she said as she took her bottom lip between her teeth.

"Well, we have that in common," I said.

"Your mom is nothing like mine. When I said my mother was crazy, I meant it. She's crazy. When I was eleven years old, I came running home from school crying because some guy tried to grab me, but I fought him off. When I told my mother about the pervert, she took me into the bathroom, grabbed the scissors and cut off all my hair. She said, 'Now men won't look at you.' I cried for at least a week," LaShaunda said.

"Why did she cut off all your hair?" I asked, completely stunned.

"I told you, she was crazy. My mom is also on drugs. No surprise there, right?" she asked.

"Who isn't on drugs these days? Every time I turn on the television, there's an advertisement for some type of drug," I said.

"You know, you're right. I've never thought about that, but those are prescription drugs, not illegal drugs," LaShaunda said with a bit of anguish in her voice.

"People get hooked on prescription drugs, too. Talk shows always have some guest who has been hooked on something," I said.

"You're keeping it real. I like that," LaShaunda said as she gave me a fist bump.

"So you never knew your father, and your mom does drugs. What else?" I asked.

"I have five younger siblings, and we had it bad. My mom refused to do anything. She wouldn't go to work, and she barely bought food. When she got her government assistance debt card for food, she'd give it away to someone in exchange for cash so that she could get her *head bad*. That's what she called it. Then, when she came down from her high, she'd try to get the drug dealers to give her something for free. When they wouldn't, she'd call the police and complain about them standing on the street corner. That just made life harder for me."

"How?" I asked.

"Hood test." LaShaunda glanced at me with a hardened expression.

"Another one?" I asked jokingly.

"Yep. When you call the Po Po on the neighborhood drug dealer, what happens when the Po Po leave?"

"The drug dealers try to find out who called the police on them," I answered.

"Exactly, and when they found out that it was my mom, they not only harassed her, but they came after me, as well. I couldn't even walk down my block without the drug dealers sending a pack of chicks after me. I've been in some brutal fights."

"Yeah, so have I," I said and paused for dramatic effect.

"So you know how to fight?" LaShaunda asked.

"Yeah, my father was an amateur boxer. He taught me a lot," I confessed, knuckling up my fists.

"That's good to know." LaShaunda paused and glanced out the window for a moment. "I tried to stay inside so that I wouldn't have to deal with fighting chicks all the time, but with no food in the house, my younger brothers and sisters looked to me to get them food."

"So what did you do?" I asked, wondering if I was prying more than I should.

"I'd sneak onto the bus and ride past downtown and into the rich suburban neighborhoods and stand outside of a grocery and beg for money and food."

"Really?" The word rushed out of my mouth.

"Yeah, really. At fourteen years old, people gave willingly. Now that I'm seventeen and look like this, they call the police on me."

"Wait a minute. So what happened with your mom? You're not living with her anymore?" I asked.

"Hell, no! She kicked me out when I was fifteen." LaShaunda shifted uncomfortably.

"Why?" I asked.

"I don't know. She just looked at me one day and said, 'Get out.' I thought she was kidding until she started pushing me out the door."

"That's crazy," I said.

"I told you my mother was crazy."

"So what did you do?" I asked.

"I did what I had to do on the streets of Milwaukee. I'm a survivor, you know. I know how to handle myself."

"Where did you sleep?" I asked.

"Wherever I could. On the rooftops of buildings, under expressway overpasses, on the corner. I'd beg for money and people would either ignore me, as if I wasn't there, or they'd give me freaking pennies. I eventually hooked up with a crew of other homeless kids. We looked out for each other. We shared food, blankets or whatever. I met people from all over that were just like me, running away from a jacked-up family. That's how I met T.J. and Bebe."

"So if you're from Milwaukee, how did you get here, in Illinois?" I asked.

"I caught a case." LaShaunda began gyrating her leg as if it were a jackhammer. I could tell she probably needed a smoke.

"What kind of case?" I asked.

"Assault. I just got fed up with the police harassing me. When you're sitting outside a business asking people for money, the police eventually come around and run you off. One particular day, I was at a gas station begging for change.

I had not eaten in three days and I was hungry. I was about to do a snatch-and-grab when the police pulled up. They asked me to move and I asked why. I didn't get an answer. They told me to go home and I was like, 'I would if I had one.' Anyway, I had my life stuffed in plastic bags. As I was picking up my stuff, one of the officers kicked it. I just snapped. I swung on him. Nailed him good, too. The cops roughed me up, but I was no stranger to violence. I knew how to protect myself from the serious hits. They took me down to the juvenile detention facility until my court date. It wasn't the worse place. I got a chance to shower every day and a bed to sleep on. As far as I was concerned at the time, being locked up was like living in Beverly Hills."

"So what happened when your court date came up?" I asked, admiring her for her strength and courage.

"The court got in touch with my mother, who showed up looking like she'd just come off of a bad high. Her hair was jacked as if she'd stuck her tongue in an electric socket. Her eyes had sunk deep into their sockets and resembled a creepy skeleton. She told the judge that she didn't want me. She said that she didn't want any of her kids. She gave the judge the contact information to my great-aunt who lived here in Chicago. My great-aunt Ola Lee took me in, but she was very old. She'd just turned eighty-five and had one foot in her grave. I moved in with her. I'd only met the woman a few times when I was a little girl. She lived in a very small apartment on the west side of the city. The place was only slightly larger than my prison cell. There was just one bed—hers—and I had to sleep with her. If you ever want to feel really creepy, sleep in the same bed with an old person. I swear, every five minutes I was waking up to make sure she had not died in her sleep."

"What was she like?" I asked.

"Her hair was as white as snow and her skin was brown and felt like Jell-O, all squishy. She couldn't stand up straight, so whenever I said anything to her, I had to squat down so she could see me. She had arthritis in her hands and feet, but I think she had it in her back, too. She tried to lay down some rules, but that didn't work. I came and went as I pleased. Then, when the winter set in and it turned cold outside, I hung around inside with her. That's when the situation got really strange. She started forgetting the simplest things. Like she'd ask me to pour her a drink of water and when I'd bring it to her, she'd say that she didn't ask for it."

"It sounds like she had Alzheimer's disease," I interjected.

"She did. I found that out when I answered her phone and spoke to a nurse at the medical clinic she went to."

"What did they say?" I asked, completely intrigued by the story she was sharing with me.

"They actually knew who I was. They said that she'd sent for me to come live with her to help take care of her. That, of course, was news to me because the last thing I wanted to do was take care of an old person."

"Maybe your mom gave the judge your aunt Ola Lee's information thinking the exchange would benefit both of you. You needed a place to stay, and she needed someone in the house with her."

"If that's what my mom called a benefit, I would have rather stayed on the street." LaShaunda looked out the window again and so did I. We were now out of the suburbs and passing through a dilapidated city neighborhood. The structures were old and worn-out looking. There were abandoned buildings and there was trash blowing everywhere.

"So what happened to Ola Lee?" I asked, bringing my thoughts back to the story she had been telling me.

"What do you think?" LaShaunda asked defensively.

"She died, didn't she?"

"Yep. It happened last winter, in January. On one of the coldest nights in the city. I remember because her apartment was drafty and the landlord didn't like to send up heat. I had to turn on the oven to keep the place warm. That was one night when I didn't mind sleeping with her. Having a warm body in the bed had its benefits. I drifted off to sleep and awoke during the night to use the bathroom. When I got back in bed, my foot brushed against hers and I said, 'Miss Ola, do you want me to get you some socks for your feet?'

"She said, 'Yeah. My feet and head are cold. The Lord is on his way to get me. Might as well have some socks on my feet when I see Him.'"

"Why did she say that?" I asked.

"She said that every night. It drove me crazy. She also slept with the Bible under her pillow. She said, 'I have my weapon, in case the devil tries to snatch me.' Anyway, I got up, went to her dresser drawer and got a pair of socks for her. 'Put them on my feet for me and get my shoes, I'm getting ready to go,' she said. I put the socks on her feet, but didn't get her shoes. I knew she wasn't going anywhere."

"The Alzheimer's again?" I asked.

"Yeah. Once I put her socks on, I crawled in bed, turned my back to her and went to sleep. Later that night I opened my eyes and sat up in bed. I noticed that Ola Lee wasn't covered up.

"'You're going to get cold again if you keep kicking the blankets off,' I said. I reached over to cover her up and when my hand touched her skin, she felt stiff, like a plank. I poked her and she didn't move. When I realized that she was dead, I freaked out. I ran out into the hallway and knocked on her neighbor's door."

"Dang, that's messed up," I said, feeling sorry for her.

"Tell me about it."

"So what did you do after that? Did she leave you any money?" I asked. LaShaunda glared at me coyly.

"No. She was dirt-poor. She didn't even have burial insurance. The Department of Family Services got involved and, the next thing I knew, I was transferred to a foster home with some of the worst people I've ever met."

"So do you live with foster parents now?" I asked.

"Yeah, and I hate those bastards, but I don't want to talk about them right now. I just want to hang out and have a good time."

"And make some money, right?" I asked with a smile.

"Damn right," she said.

eleven

MAYA

It was late in the morning, and I had been in my bedroom mindlessly surfing the internet. I read postings on Tumblr, Facebook and Twitter. Then I watched video clips from some of my favorite reality shows before I decided to waste time playing Bejeweled online.

I began to think about how perfect my relationship with Misalo was before Viviana moved in and ruined my happiness. My life seemed so different and incomplete without him. I missed the attention he gave me, our phone conversations and the great times we had shared together. It was the little things that I loved most about Misalo. Like when he'd tuck my hair behind my ear for me, the way he smiled at me and how affectionate he was. I missed holding his hand, kissing him and even the scent of him. I had to force myself to not call him, although a part of me really wanted to, but another part of me said to let him go. That was the hard part. Letting go of the guy I was deeply in love with. I felt a headache surfacing so I went into the bathroom and grabbed some aspirin. Once I took the aspirin, I laid down on my bed and drifted off to sleep.

Minutes later I awoke to the sound of my cell phone ringing. It was on my nightstand and I noticed that it was Keysha calling. I didn't bother answering it because I did not feel like talking. Once the phone stopped ringing, I turned over and tried to drift back off to sleep. I figured Keysha had called to give me an update on how her romantic day at the music festival with Wesley was going. Romance was the last thing I wanted to hear about at that particular time. A few seconds later my phone rang again. "Leave me alone," I said aloud as I curled each end of my pillow up to my ears to drown out the sound. When it stopped, I closed my eyes and went back to sleep.

Two hours later, I had been forced to get up because Grandmother Esmeralda was shaking my shoulder.

"Wake up, Maya," I heard her say as I slowly drifted back to an alert state of mind.

"What?" I asked groggily.

"Wake up, honey," I heard her insist. I stopped fighting the temptation to drift back to sleep and repositioned myself on the bed.

"Why are you waking me up, Grandma?" I asked.

"I went to Anna's fashion show and decided to come by to see the rest of my grandchildren. I have to make sure that everyone in the family is happy." *Happy? Was she serious?* I thought to myself.

"Where is Viviana?" she asked.

"I don't know," I answered.

"She did not tell you where she was going?" Grandmother Esmeralda seemed concerned.

"I don't keep up with her. She was here earlier and left with a friend. That's all I know," I said. Grandmother Esmeralda's smile turned into a straight line. At that moment my phone rang again. I got up to retrieve it from my dresser.

"I'm going to ask Paul if he knows where she is," said

Grandmother Esmeralda. She gave me a troubled glance as I watched her exit my room. By the time she was gone, the phone had stopped ringing. My mouth felt dry and I needed to brush my teeth. I decided to do that first before calling Keysha back. I was in the middle of brushing when I heard my phone buzz twice, indicating that I had just received a text message. I walked out of the bathroom with my toothbrush still in my mouth and grabbed my phone. I put in my secret code to retrieve the message.

Where are you? I really need to talk, said the text message from Keysha. I also noticed that she'd called me several times during my nap. I finished up, went back into my room and called.

"Hey," I said when Keysha picked up the phone after only one ring.

"Where have you been?" She was unquestionably irritated by my lack of availability.

"I was asleep," I said, looking in the mirror and combing my fingers through my hair. "What's up? How did your date with Wesley go?" I asked, dreading the idea of listening to her romantic outing. But, since I was her best friend, I knew that if I had not asked, she would have had an attitude.

"My date with Wesley sucked," Keysha said.

"What?" I stopped fiddling with my hair and listened.

"It was a nightmare, Maya," Keysha continued.

"I'll be right over," I said. Judging by the tone of her voice, I realized that what she had to tell me should be done face-to-face.

"I'm not at home. I'm in an emergency room."

"What! Oh, my God. What hospital? What happened? Are you okay?" I said, sitting down on the edge of my bed. At that moment I felt horrible for not taking her earlier calls.

"I'll be fine. I'm at Northwestern Hospital. It's a long story." Keysha sighed depressingly.

"Start from the beginning," I said and turned up the volume on my phone.

"Everything was going fine. Wesley picked me up and we drove downtown. He parked the car at a self-park facility near State Street by the Chicago Theater. Before heading over to the music fest, I told him that I wanted to walk down State Street toward Old Navy. Wesley didn't have a problem with it. We stopped in, and I picked up a pair of jeans and a top. I even bought a shirt for Wesley."

"That was nice of you," I said.

"It didn't cost much. The shirt was on clearance. We left Old Navy and headed over to the music fest in Grant Park. As we got closer, the sidewalks began to get jam-packed with people. At times the crowd was so thick, I could barely move. It felt creepy feeling strangers' sweaty skin on my own. Wesley suggested that we head toward Buckingham Fountain because it appeared to be less crowded, and we could get closer to the stage. I really didn't care about being close to the stage. I was just happy to be there with him. When we got near Buckingham Fountain, it was only slightly less crowded. We both complained about the heat so I told Wesley to head over to a nearby concession stand to get bottled water.

"He agreed to do that, and I watched as he mingled in with the throngs of people. As I waited, I decided to people watch as a way to kill time. That's when I saw Viviana."

"Wait, what? Viviana was at the music fest?" I wanted to be certain that I'd heard Keysha correctly.

"Yeah, I actually took out my cell phone and snapped

a few photos of her just to make sure. She didn't see me though."

"Was she there with another girl?" I asked.

"Yeah, she was. Some big girl I'd never seen before. But then it got weird. I saw Viviana do something that I didn't believe she could do."

"Keysha, spare me the Viviana details. I couldn't care less about her," I said.

"I shot a video clip of Viviana and…"

I interrupted her. "Keysha get on with the story. I don't want to hear about Viviana and her new friend who looks like a grizzly bear."

"Okay. As I put my cell phone back in my purse someone shoved me really hard, causing me to nearly fall to the ground."

"Who was it?" I asked, wondering who would do such a rude thing.

"Maya, I tell you. My heart nearly stopped when I saw who it was."

"Who?" I asked again.

"It was Toya Taylor," Keysha said.

"Toya Taylor." I paused trying to recall exactly who Toya was to Keysha. "Isn't she the girl who went shoplifting and got caught?" I asked, vaguely recalling Keysha telling me the story.

"Yes. And she looked bad," Keysha said.

"What do you mean by bad?" I asked for clarification.

"She looked rough. Like the women I see on those prison reality shows. Toya had a scar that had turned into a hideous-looking keloid. It extended downward from her right earlobe to her shoulder."

"Ewww," I said.

"That's what I was thinking, and I guess my facial expression showed it," Keysha explained.

"Well, what did she want?" I asked.

"Maya, she wanted to fight," Keysha said.

"What?" I spoke aloud.

"She had been holding a pathetic grudge against me ever since I found out who my father was and moved out of my old neighborhood. The last time I had any dealings with her was when she stole my father's Trans Am from my idiot brother, Mike."

"Wait a minute. How did Mike know Toya?" I asked, totally confused.

"That's a story for another day. Dealing with Toya was a hard lesson learned for Mike," Keysha said.

"So did you fight her?" I asked.

"Yes. I had to defend myself. She was with another girl and two guys. Toya taunted me. She griped about how I thought I was better than her ever since I learned who my biological father was and had moved to the suburbs. She told me how she had hoped she would run into me one day so that she could settle an old score. I tried to defuse the situation. I backed away from Toya, but her female friend had maneuvered behind me and shoved me into Toya. She looked at me with utter disgust. I told her that I didn't want any drama with her, but Toya had her mind set on fighting. The next thing I knew, Toya grabbed a fist full of my hair and slung me to the ground. I scraped up my hands and knees, but got right back up and lunged toward her. I was able to grab her hair and yank her fake ponytail off. Then the other girl and one of the guys grabbed and held on to me while Toya beat on me."

"Oh, my God, Keysha. This all happened in broad daylight, while there were so many people around?" I asked.

"Yeah. The time of day doesn't matter. When I lived with my mom, some of the most brazen acts took place in the middle of the day. Maya, people stood there and watched. No one was going to help. People don't like getting involved."

"What about the police? Weren't they around?" I asked.

"They were everywhere, but it was crowded and by the time the message would have reached them, the damage would have been done, and Toya and her goons would have disappeared into the crowd."

"Dang, Keysha. How badly did they beat you up?" I asked.

"Nowhere near as badly as Wesley. He had come back to help. He had wrestled the guy who was holding my arm. The boy was shorter and stockier than him. Everything happened so fast, Maya. Toya and I were fighting, and then I heard a loud hollow thud. Toya's male friends shouted for them to run and that's when I noticed Wesley lying facedown on the ground. The guy Wesley was fighting with slammed his head against the ground I think, and the blow knocked Wesley unconscious. I squatted down and rested on my knees. I turned Wesley over and placed his head in my lap.

"Was he okay?" I was now pacing the floor in my room. I couldn't believe what Keysha was telling me.

"I slapped his cheek a few times, but he didn't respond so I screamed for someone to call an ambulance. As I sat there, Wesley opened his eyes, which were blurry with confusion. I told him help was on the way. It took forever for the paramedics to find us because of the crowd. Wesley tried to get up, but he was too groggy."

"Did the police come?" I asked.

"Yeah, but by the time they got there, Toya was long gone. They took a report. After I was done with them, I got into the ambulance with Wesley and called you," Keysha said.

"I'm so sorry I didn't answer my phone," I said, feeling guilty.

"It's okay. The important thing is that Wesley is going to be all right. His dad got a neighbor to drive him to the hospital since Wesley took the car."

"I'm glad to hear that he is going to be okay. Had he not been there for you, things could have been worse," I said.

"I know. This is the second time that Wesley has come to my rescue. He's so selfless. He didn't hesitate to protect me." Keysha's voice climbed a few octaves and I immediately knew that she had gotten emotional.

"He's a good guy. There is no question about it," I said. "You're lucky to have someone like him."

"Yeah," Keysha said. I could tell there was a boulder of emotion lodged in her throat.

"When will you be back home?" I asked.

"I'm getting a ride with Wesley and his dad. When I get home, I'll give you a call," she said.

"Okay, call me then," I said and hung up.

twelve

VIVIANA

Lollapalooza was one of the biggest summer music festivals hosted by the city of Chicago. The festival featured popular alternative rock, heavy metal, punk rock and hip hop bands, dance, food and comedy performances. Thousands of music lovers from around the world came each year to enjoy the festivities. LaShaunda and I snuck into the festival by jumping an unattended section of a three-foot barricade that was normally used to keep crowds back during parades. We were not the only people who jumped the barricade during the brief moment security had stepped away. There were other partygoers who had the same idea. Once we were on the other side of the fence, we saw a sea of people dancing to the music of a rock band that neither one of us had ever heard of. The crowd was energized and totally focused on the performers, which was perfect for what I had in mind. We meandered through the crowd until I found a spot where I could talk to LaShaunda and tell her my plan.

"Here's the deal," I said, as I pulled her off the sidewalk toward a tree away from the crowd.

"What are we about to do?" she asked, while I squatted down and unzipped the backpack.

"You're going to be my drop-off girl," I answered, searching the backpack to make sure it was empty. I came across something in the bag that I pulled out.

"What is that?" LaShaunda asked loudly.

"Shhh. Girl, you have got to learn how to keep your voice down." A frown tugged at the corners of my mouth.

"Sorry, my bad. What is that?" she asked again. I flipped the switch and was surprised that it was still charged.

"A stun gun," I said, pressing the trigger. The device made a haunting crackly, buzzing sound.

"Dang. You have more rough edges than I gave you credit for." LaShaunda was clearly awestruck by the device and the fact that I had one. "Where did you get it?" she asked.

"From a girl I used to hang with. We had a big fight," I answered.

"Who won?"

"Does it really matter?" My expression hardened.

"It depends. It's like this. Growing up in Milwaukee, if I got into a fight with a chick and beat her down, I knew she would come back and with more people to get revenge. I actually saw a fight where one chick stabbed the other with a screwdriver."

LaShaunda's comment made me think about my father and the incident he had had with an attacker who had an ice pick. "Well, I doubt if I'll ever see that girl again. I don't live in the same neighborhood anymore," I said.

"Let me see the stun gun." I handed the device to her. She toyed with it for a moment and then said, "I'm going to hold on to this." LaShaunda placed the stun gun on her hip using its belt clip.

"Fine," I said, looking around to be certain that no one

was paying us any attention. I reached into the bag again and removed a smaller bag with straps that zipped up. I then began to whisper. "Okay, here is the deal. I'm a pick-pocket," I informed her.

"Sweet." She smiled.

"Most of these people are drunk or well on their way to getting drunk. I'm going to go into the crowd, get what I can and then come back out. You are going to meet me under that tree over there." I pointed to an area that was not near foot traffic. I'm going to give you the merchandise to hold. If someone tries to take it, zap them with the gun and run like hell, and then text me to let me know what went down. You do have a cell phone, right?"

"Yeah, I have one of those prepaid phones and I hate it. So be on the lookout for a better phone for me. What about you? What if you get caught?" she asked.

"I can handle myself. Besides, I won't get caught. With this many people, I can be invisible."

"That's it? That's all I have to do?" she asked.

"Yes. Just keep your cool. We'll take everything to a pawn shop that I know where they don't ask questions. We'll split the take."

"Cool." She beamed with anticipation.

The sun had started setting and LaShaunda and I were heading back to the train station. I had collected nearly $100 in cash and had swiped a respectable amount of jewelry, credit cards and other electronic devices. We laughed and talked about how we would spend our money once we sold the merchandise to the unquestioning pawn shop owner.

"So what's the first thing you're going to buy?" I asked as we crossed the intersection.

"I'm going to hook myself up with some new clothes. I'm tired of walking around in these old hand-me-downs," LaShaunda remarked.

"Yeah, I'm going to get me some new clothes, as well. I'm also going to get some nice perfume and some shoes," I said.

"Dang, I'm hungry." LaShaunda rubbed her stomach as it growled.

"There is a Subway on Michigan Avenue. Do you want to walk over there?" I asked.

"Are you treating?" LaShaunda's voice climbed an octave.

"Yeah, I got you." I beamed.

When we arrived, it was very crowded on the inside. Many of the partygoers had decided to grab something to eat before getting into their cars or catching public transportation.

"It's jam-packed in there. Why don't you wait outside and I'll go in to get our food," I suggested.

"That's cool with me. I can't stand it when people are too close to me," LaShaunda said.

"What kind of sandwich do you want?" I asked.

"Get me the Big Philly Cheesesteak with everything on it, a bag of Doritos and a Coke." LaShaunda rubbed her stomach again as if she were starving.

"Okay," I said before I stepped inside. I was glad she had agreed to wait outside. I didn't want her to catch a glimpse of the wad of cash I'd stolen and feel entitled to a percentage.

Twenty minutes later I exited Subway with our sandwiches. LaShaunda couldn't wait until we got on the train to eat. We decided to sit down on a bench outside the store. We had both finished half our sandwiches when we heard the sound of the train horn. I glanced in the direction of the train tracks, then took a quick look at my watch and realized our train was approaching.

"Damn, come on, LaShaunda. That's our train." I began running as fast as I could. The train platform was about two hundred yards in front of us, and we still had to run down several flights of steep stairs to get to the level of the platform.

"Slow down. I can't chew my food, run and carry this backpack all at the same time," LaShaunda complained.

I didn't bother to look back. My only concern was catching that train. If I could reach it, I'd stand in the doorway and hold up the train until LaShaunda arrived.

"All aboard!" I heard the train conductor shout out as I began my descent of the stairs.

"Wait!" I called out. Just as I reached the platform, the train doors closed and the train pulled off. Out of breath and exhausted, I sat down on a nearby bench. A few minutes later, LaShaunda arrived.

"Now I've got stomach cramps," she griped before releasing an odorous belch.

"Excuse you," I said and fanned the stench away from my nostrils.

"Sorry," LaShaunda said then slipped the backpack off and sat it between her legs.

"When is the next train coming?" she asked.

"In an hour. It will be dark by then. I'm going to hear about it," I said with blurry-eyed fatigue.

"Why don't we walk over to the 'L' station? We could catch it down to Ninety-Fifth Street and then hop a bus, which will take us the rest of the way," LaShaunda suggested.

"I don't know. I'm not sure if there is a bus at Ninety-Fifth Street that will take us all the way back," I said.

"Please. This city is full of bus routes. I'm sure there is a bus that will get us back before nightfall." LaShaunda sounded sure of herself.

"Are you sure?" I was more uncertain than ever.

"Tell you what. We could walk over there to the 'L' Station and ask the person in the booth if there is a bus that will get us to where we need to go. If they say no, then we'll walk back over here and wait," LaShaunda suggested. I had another idea. It was to go and hail a cab and have the driver take us home, but that would cost at least $50 and the potential of LaShaunda discovering that I was hiding cash from her.

"Okay, let's walk over to the train," I said, rising. LaShaunda picked up the backpack and we headed toward the subway station.

When we arrived, the train was sitting on the platform with its doors open.

"Come on, let's get on before it pulls off," LaShaunda said, rushing toward the doors. As soon as we stepped on, the doors closed and we took a seat. Breathlessly I said, "We didn't get a chance to ask about the bus schedule."

"We can ask once we get to the end of the line," LaShaunda said as the train began picking up speed.

"If there isn't a bus for us at the end of the line, I'll have to at least call home to let my aunt know where I am," I said, dreading the thought of explaining why I came downtown.

"Girl, I can't wait until I turn eighteen. I won't have to deal with people being in my business. You know what I'm saying?" LaShaunda asked.

"Yeah. I do. When you turn eighteen, you have total

freedom. No one is on your back. No one is trying to control your life. You can do whatever and it's cool," I said.

"Yeah, that's what it was like when I was hanging with my crew back in Milwaukee. It was hard, but we made it, you know." LaShaunda smacked her fist into the palm of her hand. I smiled, allowing the thought of pure freedom to seduce me. The train zoomed alongside the Dan Ryan Expressway for a moment before going underground. The loud roar and the jostling of the train car had begun to make me nauseous. I glanced toward the other end of the train car and noticed several people talking loudly and using every word in the book to get their point across as they crossed over from another train car into the one I was in.

"Did you hear the sound when his head hit the ground? It sounded like a coconut hitting concrete," I heard the guy say. He was the first one through the train car followed by three other people.

"It's a good thing we got out of there before the police came," I heard a female say. Her voice sounded familiar to me, but I didn't know why.

LaShaunda leaned toward me and whispered, "What's up with those fools."

I said nothing, just shrugged my shoulders as I tried to see who was behind one of the guys. They took a seat not too far from where LaShaunda and I were sitting. When I saw Toya Taylor, I gasped.

"What's wrong with you?" LaShaunda asked. I immediately turned my face away from the group and glared at the floor.

"Damn," I hissed and hoped that Toya would not notice or recognize me.

"Viviana, what's wrong?" LaShaunda's big mouth had just blown what little cover I had.

"Shhh," I said, wanting to disarm her mouth.

"Oh, hell to the no! Viviana. I know that's you!" I glanced at Toya who had decided to approach me.

"You know them?" LaShaunda asked.

"Yeah, just be cool," I said. Toya positioned herself directly in front of me. I leaned back in my seat and looked at her. She looked so much harder than I remembered. There was now a keloid scar that ran from her ear down toward her shoulder. Her teeth were far more yellow than I remembered and her lips were at least several shades darker.

"It must be ass-whipping day," she said. I knew her words were an invitation to a fight.

"For who?" LaShaunda shifted uncomfortably as Toya's friends approached us.

"What's up, Toya?" I asked, trying to be cordial.

"What's up?" Toya shouted at me is if I had called her a dirty name. "What? You think I forgot about what you and that old lady did to me? You two broads damn near blinded me when you sprayed mace in my face. It was two against one that day."

"Toya, you've got it twisted." My heart jumped in my throat.

"I got it twisted!" she shouted at the top of her voice. "I got it twisted!" she repeated herself.

"You need to calm down," LaShaunda said as she came to realize just how serious the situation was. She tried to rise, but was pushed back down by Toya's friends.

"Toya, let it go," I warned her as I knuckled up my fingers. I didn't relish the idea of getting into a brawl on the subway, but when I glanced around quickly, I noticed that several cell phone cameras were recording the argument. I knew that if we fought, footage of it would be instantly uploaded to the internet.

"Oh, so you almost take my eyesight away from me and I'm supposed to forget about that mess? Just drop it and not get justice?" The corners of her mouth had curled downward. I was about to stand up when Toya swung at me and nailed me with a solid right to my jaw. My body fell into LaShaunda's, and Toya jumped on top of me and began throwing wild punches, hitting my shoulder, my ribs and my face.

"Oh, damn!" I heard other passengers shout out. I also heard a bunch of movement. I assumed others were getting out of the way.

"Let them fight!" I heard someone who wanted the brawl to continue shout out. I managed to push Toya off me and get to my feet. I took my stance. Rage rushed through my blood as the ringing in my ear grew louder.

"Come on! Are you scared? I've learned how to fight, too." Toya's expression hardened. She tried to throw another punch, but I blocked it and caught her with two quick body shots with my right fist. Toya decided to fight dirty and she grabbed my hair. We tumbled into one of the closed doors. She pulled my hair toward the floor and rested her body weight against my back. I was in a very bad position. All I could see were shoes. I somehow managed to reach up and grab hold of her clothes and I began tugging.

"You're not so bad!" Toya taunted me. I let go of her clothing, thought about what I could do and then it came to me. I began punching her right side, below her ribs. After about ten hits, she let go and, before she could set her feet, I landed a shot to her face. Toya shouted out in pain. The next thing I knew, her goons jumped in and began punching me wildly. I stepped back, but I had nowhere to go. I covered up as they pounded my body.

"That's enough!" I heard a passenger say, but Toya and her friends wouldn't stop. I started to squat down toward the floor to avoid the sting of the punches, then I heard a crackling sound. I wasn't sure if it was from the ringing in my ear or something else.

"Oh, damn!" I heard someone howl out. Toya and her friend stopped punching me. LaShaunda must've slipped the backpack off when Toya's friends were not looking and grabbed the stun gun. She nailed a guy with it, and he hit the floor. Toya's other guy friend lunged at LaShaunda, but he was met with an electric shock to the forehead.

"It's on now!" I said to Toya as I rose up. I pummeled her for a good thirty seconds before a male passenger got involved.

"Mind your business!" I growled as I continued to work Toya over at a blistering pace. The barrage of punches had bloodied her nose, split her lip and caused a cut to begin forming above her left eye.

"Stop," the passenger pleaded. While I beat up Toya, LaShaunda had zapped Toya's third friend with the stun gun and had been kicking them while they were on the floor. When the train came to a stop, LaShaunda grabbed the backpack and yelled out, "Let's go!" Without hesitation, I rushed off the train. As I hustled down the steps I worried about how I was going to conceal my scrapes and bruises. I knew they would not go unnoticed and I didn't want to answer questions about what had happened to me. I definitely needed to come up with a quick plan.

thirteen

MAYA

"Maya, do you know where Viviana is?" My mother had walked into my room. I was in my closet sorting out my outfits and trying to determine what I would wear for the first week of school.

"I have no idea. Maybe she's run away," I said, pausing for dramatic effect.

"That's not funny, Maya. You should be just as concerned about Viviana as your grandmother and I are. I told her to come directly home and she disobeyed me." Judging by the frown upon my mother's face and the agitated tone of her voice, I knew that my mouth had nearly landed me in as much hot water as Viviana. My mother exhaled and then exited. I knew Keysha had mentioned she saw Viviana at the music fest earlier but that was hours ago.

As crazy as I realized my thinking was, I wanted to dress in such a way that I would make Misalo regret what he had done. I wanted to make other guys notice me so that Misalo would become jealous. I knew that wouldn't be too hard since everyone had probably received photos of me in my underwear. Although my photos were ancient history because I had heard, through a post on the internet, that there was a video clip circulating of a girl at my school doing a striptease. I was certain that the guys at school would be begging her to give them a private show.

"Guys," I muttered, wanting to curse the moon, the sun and the heavens. "Just when I thought I had my relationship figured out, it got ruined like mud being splashed on a white wedding dress."

By 7:00 p.m. it was dinnertime and Viviana had not returned home. Both my mom and grandmother had called her cell phone several times, but had not gotten through. I sat down to eat and couldn't have cared less about my cousin or where she was. Grandmother Esmeralda was standing at the back door, looking down the driveway for any sign of Viviana. She looked worried, as if someone had just given her bad news.

"Maya, Anna, come with me." The urgency in my mother's voice startled me.

"Where are we going?" I asked as I exhaled my annoyance about anything concerning Viviana plus interrupting my meal.

"We are going to drive around the neighborhood to see if we can find her. You two know where all the hangout spots are, so I will depend on you to direct me."

"I'll wait here in case she comes back," said Grandmother Esmeralda.

"I don't hang out like that," I said to her with a frown.

"Yes, but you still know where other kids do," my mother remarked. In my mind, having to go hunt for Viviana was just another reason for me to not like her.

Me, Anna and my mom got in her car and headed off toward a popular pizzeria. When we arrived, there were plenty of people there, but we did not see Viviana. I saw several people I knew from school, and my mom insisted that I get out and ask if they had seen Viviana.

"Mom, they don't even know who she is," I griped.

"Ask them anyway. In case they've seen her before. She's been living with us long enough for her face to become familiar with people," my mother said. Feeling embarrassed, I got out of the car and approached a group of Misalo's soccer friends.

"Hey, guys," I greeted them as I walked up to their table, which was situated outside the pizzeria at a makeshift sidewalk café.

"Hey, Maya," said Hector. He was one of Misalo's friends who had sent me a text photo of himself wearing only his boxer shorts. His message to me had said, "I can give you all this and a lot more. Misalo was stupid for letting a superfreak like you go. Come see what it feels like to be with a real man, baby." The memory of his photo made me cringe.

"You've finally come to your senses and decided to come see me?" he asked with a lustful grin.

"No, Hector. I'm not here to hook up with you. Besides, what kind of friend are you to Misalo if you got with his ex-girlfriend?" I asked.

"Hey, it's about equal opportunity. There is no shame in that," he said as he picked up a slice of pizza. The other guys he was with chuckled.

"Have you seen my cousin, Viviana?" I asked, not wanting to prolong my conversation with him.

"Your cousin? What does she look like?"

"She's about my height, wears her hair in a braided ponytail, has thick eyebrows," I explained. Hector popped his fingers.

"Isn't that the chick that Misalo hooked up with after he dumped you?" Hector asked. I felt the sting of humiliation.

"Yes," I answered quickly.

"Are you looking for her so that you can fight her? If so, can I watch?" Hector smiled, showing all his teeth. If I had the courage, I swear I would have dropkicked him to the ground.

"No. My mom and I are searching for her." I pivoted and pointed to my mom who was sitting in the car behind me. Hector stopped goofing around at that moment.

"Oh. No. I haven't seen her. Have any of you guys seen her?" Hector asked the rest of his friends. They said no.

I went back to the car and told my mother that she had not been there.

"Go by the school, Mom. Maybe she's still there testing," Anna said.

"The school is closed, honey," my mother said.

"Actually, Mom, it's probably still open. The fall sports teams are probably just finishing up practice. Maybe she decided to hang around to get to know the school," said Anna.

"Okay," my mother said and we headed off toward the school. When we pulled into the school parking lot, I saw Miss Bingham, the school librarian, walking to her car.

"Pull over there beside Miss Bingham, Mom. We can ask her, although she probably has no clue who Viviana is." I opened the car door and stepped out. I approached Miss Bingham and offered her a pleasant smile.

"Hey, Miss Bingham," I greeted her.

"Hey, Maya," she said and offered me a hug. I stepped into her embrace momentarily. "Are you ready for another school year?"

"As ready as I'll ever be," I said, looking at the school and wondering if I'd ever leave the place.

"Come on now, you have to have a better attitude than that," she said with a smile.

"I guess." I shrugged my shoulders.

"Have you been reading over the summer?" she asked.

"Yes," I said. "Keysha has, too. We spent most of the summer at the pool, which is where we did some reading."

"When school starts, make sure you and Keysha come see me. I have a bunch of new Kimani TRU books in that I know you'll like," she said.

"Okay. I will. Uhm. I have a question for you," I said, reluctant to ask.

"What is it?" She gave me her full attention.

"This is a real long shot, but I'm trying to find my cousin, Viviana. She was supposed to be up here earlier today taking some placement tests," I explained.

"What does she look like? The placement tests were held in the library earlier today. I saw everyone who came in."

I described Viviana to her.

"Oh, yes. I remember her. She was here earlier today with another girl."

"Yeah, she brought the girl you're speaking about back to our house. Do you know if they returned to the school? When they left the house later, they didn't say where they were going but I did hear that they had gone downtown."

"No, sweetie. I did not see them around the school. Once the testing was done, they left, but you know this is a big campus so they could have come back and I didn't see them. Maybe she's still downtown. Have you thought about that?"

"That could be," I said, not giving more mental energy into finding Viviana than necessary. "Okay." I turned to head toward the car.

"Hey, Maya. That girl your cousin was with. I don't know about her. She worries me."

"She can't be any worse than Viviana. Trust me on that one," I said. I got back in the car with my mother and sister.

"Miss Bingham doesn't know where Viviana went. She said that she saw her earlier when she came to take her placement test," I said as my mother continued on our mindless witch hunt for Viviana. We had been driving around aimlessly for what seemed like a hour but it was only for a few minutes. There was only a sliver of daylight left and my mother was debating on whether or not to get the police involved.

"Mom, I did hear that Viviana…"

My mother cut me off and answered her cell phone. "Hello… When did she get there?" I heard her ask. Although I couldn't hear her words very clearly, I could tell that my mother was talking to Grandmother Esmeralda and she was very upset. I heard something about the police, but I wasn't sure what that meant.

"Does she know we've been driving around looking for her?" I could tell she was upset by the way she slowed the car down and made an illegal U-turn.

"Where was she?" my mother asked. I heard my mother mumble something about Viviana being at a friend's house. I assumed she meant the girl she had brought over earlier.

"Well, I'm on my way back. Viviana and I are going to have a talk about her disappearing act when I get there," my mother said then hung up the phone.

★ ★ ★

By the time we got home, my food had gotten cold. I placed my plate in the microwave and heated it up. My mother joined Grandmother Esmeralda and Viviana in the basement for privacy. I didn't envy Viviana at that moment, but at the same time, I got twisted satisfaction knowing that she was in big trouble.

"Why can't you just leave me alone!" I heard Viviana shout out. I thought she was being overly dramatic.

"When I stop worrying about you, that's when you know that I have given up!" I heard Grandmother Esmeralda raise her voice, which was something she rarely did. The microwave chimed, so I took out my food and sat down at the kitchen table. Paul had just come into the kitchen.

"Sounds like Viviana is in a boatload of trouble," he said as he pulled back the top on a can of soda.

"Yep. She got busted. She was downtown earlier today, but that part has not come out yet," I said, unsympathetic to her crisis. There was more yelling, and this time my mother raised her voice.

"Man. What do you think they're going to do to her?" Paul asked as he sat next to me and gulped his drink.

"Hopefully, everything she has got coming to her. I should go and tell them that Keysha saw her downtown."

"You really don't like her, do you?" Paul's question surprised me. I had no idea that he had noticed the tension between me and Viviana. I always thought he was too busy with other things that thirteen-year-old boys did to notice.

"No comment," I said as I stabbed my food with my fork.

"Well, if you do tell on her, keep in mind that Mom is going to ask why you didn't mention that to her earlier and that means you'll get busted for not telling everything."

"Good point," I said.

Later that evening I was in my room on a Skype call with Keysha. She had on a pink V-neck top with short sleeves. Her hair was pulled back from her face, and I noticed a lump on her forehead above her right eye. She swiveled back and forth unconsciously in her seat, which caused the video feed to pause intermittently.

"Stop moving," I said.

"Sorry. I'm still a little shaken up," she said as she repositioned herself and brought her knees up to her chest.

"Now tell me what happened again?" I said.

"It was horrible, Maya. I was standing near Buckingham Fountain waiting for Wesley to come back with some bottled water. The next thing I knew, Toya Taylor and some other people I have never met appeared out of nowhere. Toya was looking for a fight. I knew she was a rough girl when I hung out with her, but the version of her that I saw today was grittier."

"You couldn't talk her out of a fight?" I asked.

"No. Her mind was set on beating me up. When Toya and her friends attacked me, I was shocked that no one offered to help. There were thousands of people wandering around and not a single person offered to help me."

"Except for Wesley," I reminded her.

"Yes. Wesley had my back." Keysha paused and wiped tears from the corners of her eyes.

"Are you okay?" I was concerned.

"I keep getting the flashback of Wesley's skull being smashed into the ground. It's an image and a sound I'll never forget." Keysha massaged her temples with the pads of her fingers.

"So what's the deal with Wesley?" I asked.

"They actually kept him overnight for observation. The doctors just want to make sure that he is truly okay." Keysha extended her arms above her head and stretched.

"So he'll be absent tomorrow, on the first day of school?" I asked.

"Yes," Keysha answered. "His father was kind enough to drop me at home once we picked up the car. He even came in and helped me explain what happened so my folks wouldn't freak out too badly. Then he went back to the hospital to sit with Wesley for the night. Wesley has such a cool dad. I told him that I would come over and cook for him and Wesley once he was at home."

"Wait, you're going to cook for Wesley and his father? Seriously? I never knew you could cook." I chuckled.

"I can read and follow directions. I'll figure something out." Keysha smirked.

"What are you wearing to school tomorrow?" I asked.

"I'm not sure. I just got home not too long ago. I still have to match up an outfit. What about you?" Keysha asked.

"I'm not sure, either. I had to go out on a search-and-rescue mission to help find Viviana," I explained.

"Search and rescue?" A frown formed on her face.

"Yeah, Viviana had not…" At that moment I saw Keysha's father, Jordan, come into her bedroom.

"Hang on a second, Maya," Keysha said. I watched as she spoke to her father, but I couldn't make out what they were saying. Shortly thereafter, Keysha turned her attention back to me.

"Maya, I'll talk to you tomorrow. The Chicago police are on the phone. Apparently they have more questions."

"Okay. I'll just see you at the corner in the morning at seven forty-five," I said.

"Fine. I'll see you then," she said before she terminated the chat session.

The following morning, Paul, Anna, Viviana and I were sitting at our kitchen table. We were eating waffles and bacon for breakfast before we headed out for school. My mother was really big on making sure that we ate before leaving the house. Viviana was quiet and was moving as if she were an old lady. Very slowly as if every movement caused her pain.

"What's wrong with you?" My words were sharp and cold.

Viviana paused, glared at me and said, "What do you care?"

My mother slapped her hand against the countertop. "I am sick and tired of you two bickering with each other. It's going to stop and I mean right now!" my mom snapped. She was edgier than usual and that sort of alarmed me.

"Don't make her angry, guys," said my father as he entered the kitchen and sat down. He had just come inside from picking up the newspaper off the front lawn. He was drinking coffee from his favorite cup while reading the front page.

"Daddy, why do you still have the newspaper coming to the house? By the time it arrives the news is already old," said Anna.

"I'm old-fashioned. I like holding the paper in my hands," he answered.

"Viviana, you are to come directly home after school.

You're grounded for a while," my mother reminded my cousin.

"Okay," Viviana whispered.

"What did you say?" my mother barked at her. This time my heart began to race because Mom had clearly grown very impatient with Viviana. Perhaps my mother was finally starting to see how much of a troublemaker she was, I thought.

"I said fine," Viviana reluctantly spoke loud enough to be heard. Then it happened.

"Augh! This bra is killing me," she said and began scratching her boobs.

"Ewww," echoed Paul as he watched her.

A sinful smile spread across my face. The itching powder I had placed in her bras had finally kicked in. I wanted to ask Viviana something really stupid like, "Do you have cooties?" but, given the mood of my mother, I knew not to push my luck.

"Viviana, stop that. Young ladies don't do things like that at the breakfast table. What's gotten into you?" my mother scolded.

"I just have an itch, that's all. Is it a crime to scratch myself?" Viviana's mouth was about to land her in hot water once again with my mother.

"No, but trying to break into the house is," my mother snapped.

I didn't fully understand that comment, but judging by the pathetic look that blanketed Viviana's face, I knew she had understood the comment.

"Man, you're making me feel itchy," said Paul as he began scratching his arm.

"I'm not hungry," Vivian said as she pushed herself away

from the table. She walked over to the door where she'd sat the book bag filled with school supplies that my mother had gotten for her.

"Viviana, you have to eat," my mother insisted.

"It's cool, Aunt Raven. I'm not all that hungry," Viviana said.

"Well, at least wait for Maya. She can probably help you find your way around the school."

My mother volunteered my services, which made my skin crawl.

"That's okay. I can find my own way around. Once I pick up my class schedule from the office, I'll go directly to my first class," she said as she opened the door.

"Don't forget what I said about coming home. I'm going to call to check, and you had better be here," said my mother.

"Got it," Viviana answered and walked out.

fourteen

VIVIANA

I couldn't wait to get out of the house. I didn't want to endure another lecture from Aunt Raven. I walked away as quickly as my feet would carry me without having to run. *Somewhere,* a voice in my head whispered. *Don't you wish you could run away so you'd never have to deal with them again? That would teach them a lesson about being mean to you.*

As I was crossing the railroad tracks, I felt my phone vibrate. I had just received a text from LaShaunda.

Where U at?

On my way 2 skool.

Come 2 da cafeteria when U get here.

Okay.

When I arrived at school, I walked past a row of school buses. Students had arrived and were filing into the building. It was noisy from the chatter of numerous conversations happening simultaneously. As I followed two girls into the school building, I overheard them talking about another girl named Priscilla, who was pregnant and had been forced to attend an alternative school for teen girls who were expecting. I needed to stop by the office first, but I wasn't sure how to get there from my current location.

"Excuse me," I said to a tall, skinny guy. He was sucking on a red lollipop and removed it from his mouth when he answered.

"Oh, sorry," he said, believing that he was blocking my path.

"You're not in my way," I explained. He then thought I was flirting with him. I could tell by the way his eyes traveled over my body. He was clearly trying to determine if I was worth the effort.

"What's up, *Mamí?*" he asked, trying to speak Spanish. I wasn't interested in him at all. Although Misalo was sort of off my radar now, I was still missing him and didn't want to start any kind of new relationship on the off chance that he might come back to me.

"I'm looking for the school office. Can you point me in the right direction?"

Pausing before he answered, he said, "I can do better than that. I'll walk you over there."

"Thanks."

"What's your name?" he asked, striking up a conversation.

"Viviana," I answered as we walked through the gymnasium hallway. There were framed photos of past graduates who were student athletes, along with several trophy-filled cases.

"Pretty name. My name is Mickey, but everyone calls me Red," he said.

"Why do people call you Red?" I asked, prying for more information.

"It's because of my very light skin complexion, my brown freckles and sandy-colored hair." He explained this as if it were common knowledge that all people who had similar features were nicknamed Red.

"Oh," I said, hoping I didn't sound stupid.

"What's wrong with your chest and neck?" He motioned toward my hand. I had been unconsciously scratching myself and I couldn't figure out why.

"My skin just itches, that's all."

"Maybe you should get some lotion for that. Your neck is starting to turn red," he said.

"I'll do that," I answered. We arrived at a hallway intersection and Red told me the office was down to my left.

"Nice meeting you, Viviana," he said.

"You, too, Red." I began walking away, scratching my boobs vigorously.

I had just sat down opposite LaShaunda. I glanced up at the clock on the wall and saw that I had twenty minutes left until I my first period class.

"Yo. Was that a crazy train ride yesterday or what?" LaShaunda's voice was as loud as ever. I couldn't tell if she couldn't hear well or if she had no concept of speaking softer. The drama that took place on the "L" train had excited her more than it had me.

"You fight like a man," she said.

"Yeah, I know," I said.

"Once you got it together, you beat the daylights out of Toya." LaShaunda threw a few air punches, mimicking my movements.

"She had it coming." I glanced down at my hands, which were still red and swollen around the knuckles.

"I heard a popping sound every time your fist connected," LaShaunda continued. "Then all of a sudden, the popping sounded like firecrackers going off. Pop, pop, pop, pop. You have to teach me how to throw down like that."

"Yeah. I will someday," I said and began scratching vigorously again. I thought LaShaunda would notice, but she did not.

"Girl, you're tougher than I gave you credit for. I thought for sure you would be the type of chick who'd start crying the minute Toya hit you."

"That's not me. I can take a hit."

"My crew back in Milwaukee would love you. You would fit right in. When I was hanging with them, I never had to worry about a chick like Toya running up on me. It was like, if you messed with one of us, you messed with all of us. You know what I'm saying?"

"Yeah. I understand." I paused for a moment and then said, "It was a good thing there was a White Sox baseball game going on when we were rushed off the 'L' train. I had no idea where we were or how we'd get home."

"I thought we would just wait for the next train until you pointed out all the taxicabs dropping people off at the game. That was a good call," LaShaunda said.

"I was glad you suggested that we have the cabdriver stop at the pharmacy so that I could pick up some makeup and sunglasses to hide the fact that I had gotten into a fight. I knew that my aunt Raven would freak out if she saw my face," I said, scratching myself uncontrollably.

"What's wrong with you? Stop scratching yourself like that. You're making me itch."

"I'm sorry. I'm trying not to, but I feel like the more I scratch, the more I itch. I don't know what's going on," I said as I placed my fingers under my thighs to keep myself from scraping into my skin with my fingernails.

"How did it go when you got back home? I meant to call you, but I was dealing with my own problems. I can't stand the foster parents that I live with. My foster mom's boyfriend is creepy. He makes my skin crawl."

"My aunt and grandmother blasted me. It wasn't a pretty scene," I said, giving in to the urge to scratch again.

"Damn, girl. Stop it! You've scratched so hard that you have welts on your neck." LaShaunda leaned closer to look at the damage I'd done.

"Okay," I said once again and sat on my hands.

"When I came in last night, my foster mom wasn't home. My foster dad came at me hard. He accused me of being on drugs and wanted me to come to his church so I could get help through the drug rehab ministry."

"Why does he think you're on drugs?" I asked.

"He claimed that he was a former drug addict and that he knows when someone has a problem. I told that fool my only problem was him. When I tried to walk past him and head to my room, that trick tried to grab me. I threw up my fists. The only thing that stopped it from going any further was that my foster mom pulled into the driveway."

"Seriously?" I asked.

"Yeah. That's why I need you to show me how to beat a chump down." She once again punched the air as if she were a boxer.

"I'll teach you how later," I said, scratching myself again. There was a moment of silence between us. LaShaunda stared at me as if I were diseased.

"I know your folks freaked out but did they do something to you that has you scratching like that?" she asked.

"No. I wasn't touched, but I do know that my aunt and cousins were out driving around the neighborhood looking for me," I explained.

"What? Wait. Back up. Start from the point after we covered up your battle scars with makeup and the cabdriver dropped me off at home."

"I didn't have the cabdriver pull up to the driveway. I had him drop me off at a nearby park. I made my way to the house. I knew that I couldn't go in the house with all of this merchandise in my backpack, so I climbed the fence at the rear of the property near my uncle's toolshed. Thankfully it wasn't locked, and I was able to place the backpack in there until I could come back for it. I then snuck around the side of the house and tried to enter the house through the side garage door. It was locked. I tried to force it open just so that I could get inside and act as if I'd been there for a while, but had gone unnoticed. I kicked the door hard a few times, but it wouldn't budge. My uncle thought someone was trying to break in. He went and got his gun, walked out the front door and came around to where I was."

"Your uncle pulled a gun on you?" LaShaunda's big mouth announced that to the entire cafeteria.

"Shhh," I said to her before I leaned in closer and spoke softer.

"Sorry," she said, realizing how loud she was.

"When he saw that it was me, he put the gun away and told my grandmother Esmeralda to cancel the call to the police."

"Oh, man. You were busted. Big-time," LaShaunda said as she came to realize just how serious the situation was.

"Yeah. My uncle was very upset with me for trying to break down the door. He didn't understand why I would want to do such a thing. When he asked, I couldn't give him an answer. The thought of temporary insanity was floating around in my mind though. My grandmother Esmeralda and my aunt Raven came down on me hard. My uncle wanted to jump on my back as well, but my aunt Raven assured him that she'd handle it and asked him to leave me with her and my grandmother in the basement. My aunt got in my face, pointing her finger and yelling at me. She talked about how I was disrespecting her house, myself and blah, blah, blah. My grandmother Esmeralda tried to make me feel bad by crying, and I admit watching her cry made my heart ache, but it only made Aunt Raven angrier with me. I went deep inside myself and tuned out all the shouting. I felt as if I were trying to wait for a bad thunderstorm to blow over."

"So what did they do? Did they notice your bruised face? Did they ask where you had been? Did they accuse you of things you didn't do?" LaShaunda fired off a series of questions.

"Grandmother Esmeralda accused me of having sex. She said that was the only logical explanation for my disappearance. My aunt Raven accused me of trying to destroy her home and family."

"Wow. Maybe that's why your skin is itching, perhaps it's bad nerves," LaShaunda suggested.

"I doubt it." I paused and scratched even more. "I swear, sometimes I just want to run away. Just walk out the door and leave, without ever looking back."

"I know that feeling, girl. I have it all the time," LaShaunda said sympathetically as the warning bell rang.

"When is your lunch hour?" she asked.

I pulled out my schedule and took a look. "Fifth period," I said.

"That's when mine is, as well. I'll see you then. We can eat together."

"Okay," I agreed and rose from the chair.

"What's your first class?"

"Math," I answered. "What about you?"

"Some class," she said.

"Which one?" I asked, confused.

"Here take a look." LaShaunda handed me her schedule and I noticed that it appeared to be a remedial reading class.

"The class is to help you with your reading," I said.

"I know how to read! Why do they have me in a reading class? These people around here are already trippin'," LaShaunda barked as she tried to salvage her pride.

"I know that you can read. It's probably just a mistake," I said.

"I don't want to sit in some stupid reading class. I know how to read. I can read better than all the teachers combined. I know more about stuff than they do," LaShaunda continued. She was so loud that a security guard started walking toward us.

"Here comes a security guard," I warned.

"Whatever. I can read better than they do," LaShaunda said as she moved toward the direction of her class.

Fifteen minutes into my math class, my boobs, neck and face were on fire. I could not stop scratching myself. The more I scratched, the more I itched. I felt as if there were a million microscopic ticks attacking me. Red was in my math class. He gawked at me as if I was some type of nymphomaniac. Apparently the sight of me scratching myself excited him. A few girls in the class glanced my way and offered up disgusting frowns as if I was some squalid peasant.

"Viviana?" The math teacher wanted my attention. I glanced up at him as he took off his glasses.

"Yes?" I asked, forcing myself to stop scratching.

"Are you okay? Would you like to go see the school nurse?" he asked. I was about to say no, but changed my mind.

"Yes," I said. He opened his desk drawer and began filling out a hall pass. I took it from him, but I had no intention of going to see the nurse. I was heading back home. As I walked out of the classroom and rushed down the hall, I unclasped my bra, took it off and rushed out a side door. The only thing I could think of that would cause this kind of skin irritation was a change in the laundry detergent that was being used.

When I arrived at the house, I rushed upstairs and took a shower. Afterward, I immediately felt better. I looked in the mirror and saw that my skin had turned red as fire from all my scratching. I opened the medicine cabinet in search of the hydrocortisone. I didn't see it. I checked the downstairs bathroom and the bathroom in Aunt Raven's room and didn't see it there, either. I knew we had some because I'd seen it in the medicine cabinet at least a thousand times. I walked into Paul's bedroom to see if he had been using it, then I went back to the room I shared with Anna to see if it was there, but I had no such luck. I reluctantly decided to search Maya's bedroom. I stood in the center of her bedroom and scanned the surfaces. I moved over to her dresser where she kept her perfume and saw something. It was positioned behind her jewelry box. There were several blue packets of itching powder and the tube of hydrocortisone. I then began thinking.

"Why would Maya have done this?" Out of pure curiosity, I opened the itching powder and placed a little on my forearm and rubbed it in with the pads of my fingers. Sure enough, I began itching like crazy. I then immediately went back into the bathroom and washed it off. I returned to the bedroom I shared with Anna, opened up my underwear drawer and pulled out another bra. This time I inspected it and that's when I saw the white powder in the cups. Maya had placed itching powder in all my bras.

"Ahhhhh!" I yelled out. My scream hung in the air. Then in a moment of blinding-white rage, I marched back into her room and grabbed the rest of the itching powder she'd purchased. I spread it on her pillows and blankets. I unscrewed the caps on the lotion she used and sprinkled some in there. I unscrewed her shampoo and conditioner bottles and sprinkled some there, as well.

"Now it's her turn to look like a freak," I said as I walked out of her room.

fifteen

MAYA

I had killed thirty minutes at the school library searching for an interesting book to read. I then decided to hang around the building after school and wait for Keysha, who had a theater club meeting. She had said the meeting would only take half an hour. I had just entered the auditorium and taken a seat down near the stage. I listened as dates for the fall play tryouts were announced. Once they had finished up, I joined Keysha and we walked out together.

"So what's the fall play going to be this year?" I asked as I allowed her to exit the auditorium first and enter the rest of the complex as we headed to the buses at the main entrance.

"*A Christmas Carol* by Charles Dickens," Keysha said.

"Do you think you'll get the lead role?" I asked.

"That would be interesting, seeing as how Scrooge is a male. I could probably pull it off with the right costume and some really good makeup."

"But then you'd have to walk around practicing speaking like an old stingy man," I said, laughing out loud.

"You're right. I was actually thinking of shooting for the role of the Ghost of Christmas Past but right now everything is still in the preplanning stage. I'm not sure that I'm going to try out this year. I just wanted to get information,"

Keysha said as we exited the building and stepped out into the light of the sunset.

"Have you spoken to Wesley?" I asked.

"I got a text from him earlier. He said that he was being released."

"That's good," I said.

"Are you going to be in any activities this year?" Keysha asked.

"I'm not sure what I'm going to do this year. If something interests me, I'll let you know," I said as we walked across the school parking lot.

"Have you talked to Misalo since history class this afternoon?"

"No. I can't believe that he is in our history class," I said.

"What I can't believe is that your cousin, Viviana, is in my honors English class and in our history class."

"Viviana is in your honors English class? That has to be a mistake. The girl can barely read a street sign," I said.

"Well, if it was an error, I'm sure administration will catch it. Maybe that explains why she wasn't in class today," Keysha said. "Why she didn't answer roll call."

"Well, I know she came to school, which means she either ditched class or that administration caught their error and placed her into a basic English class," I suggested.

"But that would not explain why she missed our history class, too," Keysha reminded me.

"It's not my job to worry about whether or not she comes to school. I couldn't care less about her." I was tired of devoting so much energy to the whereabouts of Viviana.

"Are you going to tell your parents that she wasn't in class today?"

"No. They'll send a letter home. She can explain then," I said.

"Well, I'm going to head toward Wesley's house. I just want to make sure he's okay," Keysha said.

"So what's up with you two? Is it official? Is he your boo thang now?" I asked.

"For now we're just good friends still."

"What are you going to do if Lori comes back?" I asked.

"If he even thinks about saying so much as hello to her, then it's over. We are very clear about Lori."

"Just checking," I said and left the subject of Lori and Wesley alone.

When I got home, Viviana was sitting at the kitchen table reading a social studies book. She briefly glanced up at me with hate ablaze in her eyes.

"Why weren't you at school today?" I asked, just to be meddlesome.

"I was at school," she answered.

"You weren't in second period history or third period English," I said just to let her know that I knew she had cut two classes.

"Who are you? *Harriet the Spy?*" Viviana asked condescendingly.

"You're right. What do I care." I chuckled and walked past her.

"Hey, Maya. Are you going to your room?"

"Yes. I'm going to chill out on my bed and do my homework."

"Cool. Don't let the bedbugs bite," she said and laughed at me as if she knew something I didn't.

I entered the bedroom and glanced around. I noticed

that my laundry hamper was full and decided to do a load. I stood at my dresser and removed my jewelry. That's when I noticed that the remaining itching powder packets were missing. I had stupidly left them out in plain sight. I had meant to get rid of what I didn't use. Then I realized what Viviana had meant when she had said don't let the bedbugs bite. I walked over to my bed and tossed back the comforter. I noticed the white powder on my purple sheets. Viviana had poured the itching powder on my bed. Then it dawned on me that she had probably missed class because she was itching. The thought of that made me smile.

I yanked all the sheets off the bed and took them down to the laundry room. Just before I was about to go into the basement, I stopped on the main floor and said, "Viviana, I'm about to wash my bedsheets. Do you have anything in the washer?"

"Why are you washing your bedsheets?" She rose from the kitchen table and positioned herself where I could see her.

"I like fresh sheets," I said with a knowing grin.

"No. I don't have anything in the washer," she said and went back to her seat.

I smiled. I got nothing but joy out of letting her know that her prank had backfired. While my sheets were washing, I decided to take a shower. When I finished, I came back into my room, grabbed my scented lotion and began oiling my skin. I applied a healthy amount to my legs, arms and torso. I put on my pajamas and then headed down to the kitchen for something to drink. As I walked into the kitchen, I scratched the top of my hand. I pulled a glass down from the cupboard and filled it with crushed ice from the refrigerator.

"Did you take a shower?" Viviana asked.

"Yes. Why?" I asked.

"Did you wash your hair?"

"No," I said, feeling as if she were prying. I filled my glass with water and headed out of the kitchen. Then it hit me like a blast of cold winter air. I began itching everywhere. Stomach, arms, legs, neck. I began twitching and dancing in place.

"What's wrong with you?" Viviana asked with an evil smirk.

"Ahhh, damn!" I yelled and dropped my glass of ice water. It shattered on the floor near my feet. I began scratching everywhere. My hands could not move quickly enough nor could my fingers be all over my body at the same time.

"Ahhhh," I screamed out again as I pranced around wildly like a cowboy trying to ride a bull at a rodeo.

"It doesn't feel so good does it, Maya?" Viviana barked at me viciously.

"What did you do?" I cried out.

"The same thing you did to me, only worse."

"I hate you, Viviana," I screamed at her.

"The feeling is mutual," she snarled back.

I ran back upstairs.

"By the way, we're out of hydrocortisone. You'll have to go to the drugstore to get more," she said, snickering. As I took another shower, I realized that not only had she placed the powder on my bed, but also in my lotion. I knew right then that I had to get rid of all my personal care products and wash every item of clothing I owned.

Keysha and I had just walked into our history class. We sat across from each other and began talking. The teacher,

Mr. Morgan, had not entered the room yet. Wesley walked in and sat behind Keysha. There were a few stitches at the back of his head that Keysha and I both took a look at.

"Hold your head down," Keysha said to him as he sat. Wesley rested his head on his forearms. Keysha and I hovered above to get a closer look.

"Does it hurt?" I asked.

"No. It's just a little tender and it itches," he said.

"Please stop talking about itching," I said, having a bad flashback. I had told Keysha earlier about what I'd done to Viviana and how she had gotten even with me.

"It's a good thing you have a thick skull," Keysha said. Wesley sat upright and lightly touched the back of his head. A few moments later Misalo walked into the room. He wasn't there yesterday, but I had heard through the grapevine that he had been at the doctor's office getting his annual physical. He looked at me briefly and said hello.

"Hi," I answered. He walked past me and sat in my row all the way at the back of the room. Shortly thereafter, Viviana entered the room. She looked around, confused as to where she'd sit.

"Yo, Viviana. You can sit next to me," said a boy named Red. Viviana looked around for another seat, but she didn't have much choice since nearly all the seats had been taken. She walked over and sat next to him, and he stared at her as if he were undressing her.

Finally Mr. Morgan walked into the room. He was an older black man in his sixties. His hair was a mixture of black and gray and he had a protruding belly about the size of an inflated beach ball. He had to constantly pull up his pants. Keysha and I had joked that if he pulled them up any higher his belt would end up in his armpits.

Yesterday he had told the class a story from his years as an undergraduate student at Kent State University in Ohio and how he had protested the Vietnam War. He told the sad story of how several college students were killed by the National Guard. For the benefit of those who were not in his class yesterday, he retold the story.

"So when we get to that part of American history, I'll be more than happy to share my thoughts on it because I lived through it," said Mr. Morgan. I noticed that Viviana had raised her hand.

"What's your name?" asked Mr. Morgan.

"Viviana," she answered.

"Do you have a question?" he asked.

"No. I just wanted to say that my grandfather served in Vietnam," Viviana offered.

"Really? What branch of the military was he in?" asked Mr. Morgan.

"Uhm." Viviana paused. I could see that she was trying to remember. Then she slowly answered. "The army."

"Did he come back home?" asked Mr. Morgan.

"Yes, but he passed away before I was born," she said.

"I'm sorry to hear that." Mr. Morgan thought for a moment then said, "Okay, I teach history a little differently. I like to make it fun and interesting. Most of all, I don't want to teach you how to retain information just to pass a test. What I want to do is teach you the information so that it stays with you all your life. So what I would like to do is determine how much history you already know." Mr. Morgan walked behind his desk and pulled down the black-and-white projector screen. There was a cart with an LCD projector with a laptop computer hooked up to it. He turned on the machines and an image popped onto the screen.

"How many of you are familiar with a game called *Jeopardy!?*" he asked. Viviana and Misalo were the only people who raised a hand. Mr. Morgan looked around.

"I see. Only two people are," he said. "Here is what I want to do. Viviana is going to represent the right side of the room, and what's your name, son?"

"Misalo."

"Okay, Misalo, you're going to represent the left side of the room. I want both of you to come up front. What I have projected on the screen is the *Jeopardy!* game board. There are three categories. Civil War, American Literature and American Music. I've kept the game very simple. The questions are worth either one hundred points or two hundred points. Viviana and Misalo, if you don't know the answer, you can ask a team member if they know. You'll have fifteen seconds to provide me with an answer. If you give the wrong answer, you will be in the hole for the amount of points you attempted to get. Once you've had your turn, another member from each team will come up for a chance to play. Do you understand the rules?"

"So let me get this right. If I say American Music for two hundred, and I get it wrong, I'll be two hundred points in the hole?" Misalo asked.

"You got it. But, if you give the correct answer, you'll be up by two hundred points."

"Okay, I got it," said Misalo.

"Viviana, we'll start with you. Pick a category and a point amount."

"I'll take American Literature for two hundred," Viviana said. I could tell she was hoping that she wouldn't get a question that was too hard.

"Samuel Clemens is a beloved American author. However, he did not publish books under that name. For two hundred points, tell me the name he published his books under," said Mr. Morgan. Viviana looked nervous. Then her eyes lit up and I could tell she'd come up with an answer. I was eager to laugh at her when she got it wrong.

"Uhm," she stalled.

"She'll never get this. I don't even know why she's trying," I whispered to Keysha.

"Do you want to ask your teammates for help?" asked Mr. Morgan. She briefly turned and looked at Red to see if he could help. He shrugged his shoulders, indicating that he had no clue.

"Uhm, I'm going to say—" she paused and then slowly answered "—Mark Twain."

"That is correct. Your team now has two hundred points," said Mr. Morgan. She exhaled a sigh of relief. I chalked up her correct answer as pure luck.

"Misalo, your turn," said Mr. Morgan.

"American Music for two hundred points," he said. I could hear the competitiveness in his voice. "You're going down," he told Viviana.

"The inventor of rock and roll sang a song called 'Johnny B. Goode.' What is the inventor's name?" asked Mr. Morgan.

"Aw, man, why are you giving out such hard questions? Can't you give questions from this century?" whined Misalo.

"It's called *history,* not today's news," answered Mr. Morgan.

"Uhm, a little help please." Misalo turned toward me with pleading eyes.

"It's Elvis Presley. Duh!" I said.

"It's some guy named Richard Little," I heard another student on my team blurt out.

"It's Chuck, uhm, uhm." Keysha was popping her fingers trying to remember the person's last name. "Berry."

"Time's up, Misalo. What's your answer?" asked Mr. Morgan.

"Elvis Presley," Misalo said with absolute confidence.

"Wrong," said Mr. Morgan. Misalo's chest deflated. "The correct answer is Chuck Berry."

"I told you it was Chuck Berry," Keysha barked at Misalo.

"Viviana?" Mr. Morgan looked at her. "You may sit down."

"Oh," she said. Apparently she had forgotten to let someone else from her team play. The next two players that came up were Keysha and Red. Keysha went first.

"I'll take Civil War for two hundred," she said.

"The Civil War had a general for the northern part of the country and a general for the southern part. Name the two generals."

"Ulysses S. Grant and Robert E. Lee," Keysha quickly answered the question. My team was now back to zero instead of negative two hundred.

"Red, it's your turn," said Mr. Morgan. Red brushed his fingers across his lips before he said, "American Music for one hundred points."

"At the turn of the twentieth century, this music composer was known as the King of Ragtime Music. What is the name of the musician?" asked Mr. Morgan. Red dropped his bottom jaw to his chest and looked dumbfounded, as if Mr. Morgan were speaking a foreign language. Red didn't bother to ask his team for help. He just blurted out what was inside his empty head.

"Drake," he said.

"Drake is incorrect. Your team now has only one hundred points," said Mr. Morgan. My side of the room battled back and forth with Viviana's side. I was surprised that I actually knew the answers to several of the questions. However, there were plenty that I was clueless about. At the end of class, my side won because I had given the correct answer to an American Literature question.

When the bell rang, Keysha and I headed out the door.

"Maya, wait a minute," Misalo called out. I waited for him in the hallway. Keysha couldn't stay because she had to get to her honors English class on the other side of the school.

"Good job," Misalo said as he came out of the room and smiled at me.

"Excuse me," I said to Viviana as I looked over and noticed that Viviana was trying to squeeze past. Red was on her heel, attempting to put his moves on her. Misalo stepped out of the way so they could walk on by. He briefly glanced at Viviana. The expression on his face was a sour one.

"Thanks," I said to Misalo and turned to leave. I was happy that he had finally taken off his blinders and seen Viviana's true colors. I walked away and he followed me.

"Would you like to get something to eat after school?" he asked.

"I've got plans," I said, wanting him to know that getting back with me wasn't going to be as easy as asking me for a lunch date. Although I still had strong feelings for him, I wasn't about to allow him to snake his way back into my heart so easily.

"Maybe some other time then." He sounded pathetic.

"Not until I get a sincere apology from you, Misalo."

"I'm sorry, okay. Is that good enough?" He stopped walking. I looked over at him and studied his eyes. I did not see sincerity anywhere. What I did see and hear was an attempt to appease me so I would let my guard down.

"No," I said and walked away.

sixteen

VIVIANA

Admittedly, even though my team had lost, I had had fun in class. I particularly liked the game Mr. Morgan had us play. I knew that his class would become one of my favorites.

"What other things do you like besides school?" Red walked alongside me as I headed toward my English class, which was taught by Miss Shaheen according to my schedule.

"Why do you care?" I glanced at Red who seemed surprised by my coldness.

"I'm curious about you. Is that a bad thing?" he asked.

"I don't know. You tell me. Is it?"

"Well, I hope not. When is your lunch hour?" he asked.

"Why?"

"Well, I thought we could sit together and talk," he said.

"I already have someone I talk to during lunch."

"Oh, you have a boyfriend? What's his name, maybe I know him," Red kept prying.

"Red, you should just give up now. I am not interested in you," I said more directly.

"Oh, it's like that?" he said. I could tell I had stepped on his ego.

"Look. I just got over a bad breakup, and I'm not interested right now." I offered him a crumb of information as a gesture of kindness.

"He must be a real idiot to break up with a girl as pretty as you," Red said, continuing his efforts to win me over.

"The relationship was complicated," I said.

"What relationship isn't?"

"So you're a relationship expert?" I mockingly asked.

"I have older sisters who have gone through some nasty breakups."

"Well, I am positive their experience was nothing like what I have been through," I said as I opened the door to my classroom.

"So can we hang out after school or something?" Red asked as the tardy bell rang.

"Goodbye, Red," I said as I entered the room.

I found an empty seat just as Miss Shaheen began taking attendance. When she called my name, she paused and asked me to come up to her desk.

"I wonder what this is about," I muttered softly.

"You weren't here yesterday," she said.

"Yeah. I had sort of an emergency I had to deal with," I said without explaining my whereabouts or what the situation was.

"There is a strict attendance policy for honors classes," she explained. "If you miss another class without an excuse, it could impact your grade."

"Okay," I said, not giving what she had said any more thought. I was about to head back to my desk when she stopped me.

"Yesterday I gave out a reading assignment. We are read-

ing *Oedipus Rex* by Sophocles. You'll need to start reading it. This is not a class you can afford to fall behind in."

I shrugged my shoulders and said, "Okay."

By the end of the day, I was loaded with homework.
The books I'd been given were thick and in my mind were
equivalent to carrying a sack of boulders around. The load
felt heavy enough to snap my spine, I thought. LaShaunda
sent me a text message and asked me to wait for her after
school. She had a meeting with her writing teacher. Yesterday she had mentioned that her writing teacher had ticked
her off because she took a red pen to a paragraph she was
asked to write. LaShaunda had said the teacher told her that
she had poor speech and grammar skills that needed to be
addressed.

I decided to multitask by going to the school library
where I could get a start on my homework. I loved learning and had the ability to soak up information and retrieve
it whenever I needed to. I loved reading, too. My grammar school library was filled with books, and I spent an
enormous amout of time there, before and after school.
My mother would drop me off an hour early sometimes so
that she could go do whatever she had to take care of. She
treated teachers as her personal babysitters. At least that is
what I heard some teachers say about her in hushed whispers.

On days when it was raining or too cold, the school librarian took pity on me and allowed me inside the building
before the school opened. She did it at the risk of getting in
trouble. She told me that as long as I was quiet, she didn't
mind. I was just happy to be out of the miserable weather.
I would sit Indian style on the carpeted floor in one of the
book aisles and read at random. During those days, I loved
the R. L. Stine books—the scary ones. When I got bored

with those types of books, I began reading autobiographies. I read *The Life and Death of Crazy Horse* by Russell Freedman. After that it was *Surviving Hitler: A Boy in the Nazi Death Camps*. Then I began to realize how limited my school library was.

When I stayed with Grandmother Esmeralda, we would go to the local city library for one reason or another. Sometimes she picked up tax forms. Another time she took a basic computer skills class, and later she took a memoir writing workshop. She had said that she needed to write her life story so that future generations would remember our history. While she did those things, I found something to read to pass the time.

I sat down at one of the large wooden tables and removed my English book. Just before I began reading, I noticed that Keysha was sitting at a table not too far from me. She was looking at me oddly, as if something about me had her completely perplexed. I ignored her and focused on my assignment.

Twenty minutes later, LaShaunda startled me by slamming her folders on the table.

"I hate this school and these damn teachers!" She was breathing heavily as if she'd been running from someone.

"What's wrong? What happened?" I asked, concerned.

"This school, these teachers, everything. People around here are trying to treat me like I am dumb. I am not dumb. I'm smart. I know how to survive in the streets where real life happens. None of these dumb-ass educated teachers around here could survive one night on the streets. Girls like you and me, Viviana, we know what life is about. We know what it's like to struggle and survive. You and I have street knowledge, and that's the best teacher in the world.

All of these teachers around here can stick it where the sun can't shine. You know what I'm saying?"

"Yeah, I understand." I agreed with her.

"I don't see how knowing what a preposition does will help me make money. Like some employer is really going to interview me and ask me what does a preposition do. This place is stupid, stupid, stupid! What they need to be teaching is some real life stuff, you know what I'm saying?" LaShaunda continued her tirade. In my mind I thought about what a preposition does and recalled that prepositions are words that connect or relate nouns and pronouns to preceding words and phrases.

"Come on. Let's go," I suggested before the librarian came along and asked LaShaunda to lower her voice. If that happened, I feared LaShaunda would become even more enraged. As we walked home, she asked me about the merchandise we'd stolen a few days earlier.

"So what's the deal? When are we going to go pawn that stuff and get the cash, and when will you give me one of the new phones you took—I may not be able to turn it on but I can at least have a phone that takes pictures," she continued, gesturing with her hands.

"I told you. I'm grounded right now and can't leave the house. My aunt and uncle have me on a short leash."

"Tell them to go to hell! You got business to handle."

LaShaunda assumed that I could do or say anything to my aunt and uncle without fear of consequences. Sure, I didn't like living there, but I wasn't ready to tell either of them to go jump off a bridge, at least not yet.

"Just relax. We'll get the money for the merchandise. You have to trust me."

"I need money, Viviana. I'm going crazy living in the

house with my foster mom and her boyfriend. That guy looks at me and I can tell that he's undressing me. I swear, if that fool touches me, I'm going to commit a homicide." She made a fist with one hand and slapped the palm of her other one.

"Why don't you call the social worker and report him?"

"Those social workers don't care! I'm just a damn case number to them and a check to my foster mom. By the time my social worker gets around to dealing with this, an entire school year will have gone by. They're slow. As long as I haven't been shot, raped or part of a felony, they're not going to do much to rock the boat," LaShaunda argued.

"What do you need the money for?" I asked. LaShaunda stopped walking, then turned to look at me.

"Look at my clothes, Viviana. I'm walking around the school wearing stuff from the 1980s. My foster mom only shops at thrift stores. Even if I had grown up in the 1980s I would not have been caught dead wearing leg warmers. I'm not trying to look like Madonna. Lady GaGa has already taken that job. Besides, I need to buy me some personal stuff because my foster mom uses whatever from the Stone Age, and the granny panties that she buys makes me feel like I have on a giant diaper."

"Oh," I replied, picking up on what she meant. "I have about twenty bucks. Take it and do what you need to do. You don't have to pay me back," I said, reaching into my purse and handing her the money.

"Seriously? You're just going to give me twenty dollars?" She seemed both surprised and pleased.

"It's the least I can do for you helping me out when I was being attacked by Toya," I said with a smile.

"You're all right with me," LaShaunda said and bobbed

her head approvingly. We had just turned a corner and began walking down a side street. "Look, I got this crazy idea that I'm working on, that I want you to be part of."

"What?" I asked.

"I can't tell you right now because I'm still working out all the details. But, if I could show you a lifestyle where you could live freely and not worry about people trying to run your life, would you be interested?"

"God, yes," I said, hoping she'd tell me more.

"Okay. I'll fill you in when the time is right." She grinned at me.

"Cool. I'd better get into the house."

"Yeah. I'm going to head up to the pharmacy. Peace." She tossed up two fingers.

seventeen

MAYA

Keysha and I were walking up the back stairwell. We were headed to our history class. When we made it to the second floor, I noticed that the hallway seemed noisier than usual. The sound of books being dropped on the floor was a constant sound, as well as the sounds of locker doors slamming and a thousand voices talking all at once.

"You know the homecoming dance is coming up in October," Keysha said.

"And," I responded, wanting to know why she had brought up the subject.

"Well, I'm sort of hoping Wesley will ask me to go."

"Oh, I'm sure he will. Especially now that he is back on your good side," I said.

"Do you think I should give him a hint, you know, just to make sure he asks?"

"That's up to you." I thought about Misalo. "Misalo asked me out to lunch yesterday."

"Really? Are you going?"

"No. I told him that I would not go until I got a real apology from him," I said.

"What would he have to do for you to believe and forgive him?"

I thought about her question for a moment. "Say that he's sorry and promise he will never treat me like crap again, and really mean it."

"Maybe you should tell him that. You know guys are really clueless when it comes to stuff like that."

"How do you know how boys think?" I questioned her.

"I spent hours at the swimming pool reading books and articles on guys and relationships, remember." She chuckled sarcastically as we entered our classroom. We took our seats and I took out my heavy history book. "Look at that." She pointed to a message that Mr. Morgan had written on the blackboard.

"Win ten thousand dollars in prizes and scholarship money," I repeated, reading what was written on the board.

"What do you think that is?"

"I have no idea," I said, repositioning myself in my row. Mr. Morgan entered the room and shut the door behind him. As he walked toward his desk, he took a sip of the coffee he carried in a mug and then took a seat. He began taking attendance. Once that was done, he explained the message on the blackboard.

"I wanted to bring to everyone's attention that tryouts for the High School District Quiz Show Team are now open," he said.

"What's that?" asked Viviana.

"Duh! It's a quiz show," I said, not wanting to pass up the opportunity to bruise her self-esteem. She glanced at me, and I saw the flames of revulsion flickering in her eyes.

"It's a quiz show," Mr. Morgan continued. "Four students will have a chance to represent Thornwood High School in the district competition. If our team wins the district competition, each student will receive twenty-five hundred dollars in scholarship money and advance to the regional competition. If we win the regionals, then each student will receive five thousand dollars in scholarship money and a new laptop computer, and then we advance to the national competition. The final show will be hosted by a Hollywood celebrity."

"Ooh! Who?" asked Red from across the room.

"Let's see." Mr. Morgan opened a folder that was on his desk and glanced at it.

"Last year's host was a guy named Common," he said.

"Ooh! We get to meet Common?" asked Viviana.

"No, you won't get to meet Common because you'd never make the team." I took another shot at her.

"Well, that makes two of us," she fired back.

"Ladies, cut it out," Mr. Morgan warned us before he continued. "Last year Thornwood made it to the regionals, but lost to a high school from Cleveland, Ohio."

"So how do you try out?" asked Keysha.

"Tryouts will be held tomorrow after school in the auditorium. Those of you who are interested, please come. There will be a mock show set up similar to what we did in class yesterday. The top four students will make the team."

I leaned in closer to Keysha and whispered, "Are you thinking about trying out?"

"Yes."

"Why?" I asked.

"It seems like a lot of fun. Besides, I have all of this useless information I've been storing in my head. I might as well put it to good use, and it would be something different."

"So you're not going to try out for the school play?" I asked.

"The quiz show sounds more exciting," Keysha said. "Excuse me, Mr. Morgan." Keysha raised her hand.

"Yes, Keysha," he acknowledged her.

"Where will the competitions be held?" she asked.

"There will be eight district competitions that will be held within area high schools. Regionals will be held in Cincinnati, Ohio, and nationals will be held in Washington, D.C. Did I mention that the top schools will also get a tour of the White House?"

"Really!" I squealed and clapped my hands in delight.

"For those who make the team, practice sessions will be held after school in the library for one hour. Please raise your hand if you plan to try out for the show," instructed Mr. Morgan. I glanced around the room. Keysha's hand was raised, and so were Viviana's and Red's. A few other students had their hands raised, as well. To my utter shock, when I looked at the back of the room, I saw that Misalo's hand was also up. Our eyes met and he winked at me.

"Get a life," I muttered softly.

"Raise your hand," Keysha insisted.

"I'm not sure if I want to do it," I said.

"Think about it. If you and Misalo make the team, you'll see more of each other," Keysha pointed out.

"That is very true," I agreed and raised my hand to be counted.

The following day after school, Keysha and I walked over to the auditorium. I had no idea if I should try out, but at the same time I was excited about participating. As we walked down the hall toward the auditorium, I heard someone call my name. I turned around and saw Misalo and Wesley approaching.

"Oh, God," I grumbled.

"Are you heading over to try out for the show?" Misalo asked.

"Yes," I answered.

"Hi, Maya," Wesley greeted me as he leaned toward Keysha and playfully bumped his shoulder against hers.

"Hi, Wesley," I said as I kept moving forward.

"Do you think you'll make the team?" Misalo asked.

"I don't know," I answered. "So why aren't you with Viviana?" I knew my question would sting before I asked. A remorseful look spread across Misalo's face. He didn't say anything and I knew that he had lost any words he had prepared to speak in his mouth.

"I've moved on, Maya," he answered. "I'm sorry for everything I've done to hurt you. I was dumb. I was stupid and I was stubborn." Misalo walked ahead of everyone to pull open and hold the door for us. As I walked past him, I began to believe that the words coming from his mouth were sincere. After we signed in, we all took seats in the third row back from the stage. A few minutes later, I saw Viviana walk in with LaShaunda, who was wearing a baseball cap, baggy blue jeans and an oversize shirt.

I craned my neck and whispered to Keysha, "Hood rat alert."

"Please tell me that when I first moved out here that I didn't look like her." Keysha pointed to LaShaunda.

Chuckling, I said, "You were just rough around the edges. That chick has jagged edges." As I glanced around the auditorium, I counted eighteen students. I knew then that making the team would not be an easy task.

"Okay, let me have your attention." Mr. Morgan took center stage. He adjusted his slacks, took a deep breath and began. "Thank you for coming to the tryouts. Everyone will be called up to the stage individually and will be asked four questions worth ten points each. The questions will be on various topics. Once you've answered the questions, you are free to go. Only four students will make the team. In the event of a tie, those students with the highest scores will come back for another round, and a winner will be determined. Any questions?" No one raised their hand. "Okay. I've taken the sign-in sheet, and I'm just going to go down the list."

We sat and listened as students tried to answer some very tough questions, many of which I didn't know the answer to. Keysha and Misalo knew a few, but that wasn't very comforting.

"Viviana," Mr. Morgan called. I glanced in her direction and noticed that her friend, LaShaunda, looked as if she were about to doze off to sleep. Clearly this wasn't her idea of fun. Viviana walked onto the stage and stood in front of the judges. The librarian asked the first question.

"'Call me Ishmael' is the first line of what Herman Melville novel?" she asked. Viviana paused and shifted her eyes several times as she searched her mind for the answer.

"Moby-Dick," she answered.

"Next question. What television visionary created the hippest trip in America, *Soul Train?"* Again, Viviana paused and searched her mind for the answer. She kept tapping her hand against her thigh like a nervous jackrabbit.

"Don Cornelius," she answered.

"Next question. Of the four presidents carved into Mount Rushmore, who is the only one depicted with a mustache?"

Misalo leaned closer to me and whispered, "Teddy Roosevelt."

"How do you know that?" I asked.

"I had to write a paper on him," he explained.

"By the way, I meant to ask you. How are you going to play soccer if you make this team?"

"I'm not playing this year," he answered.

"Really? Why?"

"Doctor's orders. I have iliotibial band syndrome," he said.

"What is that?"

"Knee and hip problems. They're old injuries that have flared up," he said and then nodded toward Viviana who still had not answered the question.

"Uhm," Viviana stalled. "Roosevelt, the first one, not the second one."

"Okay. Final question. Charles Darwin is buried next to Sir Isaac Newton in what famous London cemetery?"

"Do you know the answer?" Keysha asked.

"I have no idea," I admitted. "Do you?"

"Yes," she answered.

"Okay, are you like a genius or something? How do you know this stuff?"

"I told you. My head is filled with all types of crazy information. I'm not sure how it all got there."

"Westminster Abbey," Viviana answered.

"Was that the right answer?" I asked Keysha.

"Yes," Keysha said.

"Jeez," I said sarcastically.

"Okay, Viviana, you may go," said Mr. Morgan. Viviana walked back to her seat, woke up her friend and then left.

"Keysha, your turn," said Mr. Morgan.

"Wish me luck," Keysha said.

"You'll do fine," I assured her. Just as Viviana had done,

Keysha took center stage and waited for the questions to be asked.

Mr. Morgan asked, "What is the largest denomination of U.S. currency in circulation today?"

"The one-hundred-dollar bill," Keysha answered.

"Next question. What queen sponsored the transatlantic voyage of Christopher Columbus?"

"Queen Isabella," Keysha answered.

"Next question. What *30 Rock* star wrote the book *Bossypants?*"

Keysha paused and then slowly said, "Tina Fey." I could tell she wasn't certain of her answer.

"Last question," said Mr. Morgan. "In 1960, what singer caused a national craze with his hit song, 'The Twist'?"

"Uhm." Keysha paused then began snapping her fingers hoping an answer would come. "Little Richard," she answered.

"No. The correct answer is Chubby Checker. Thank you, Keysha. You may go."

Twenty minutes later I walked out of the auditorium with sweaty palms. Keysha was waiting for me in the hallway and asked how my round went.

"That was hard," I complained as we walked toward an exit.

"Tell me about it. I felt like my brain froze up," said Keysha.

"The questions made me feel like I didn't know anything," I said.

"What questions were you asked?" Keysha said.

"Well, I know that I got one of them right. I was asked what the name of Spider-Man's alter ego is. I was like, duh, Peter Parker. Then Mr. Morgan switched and asked, 'In what film does Marlon Brando say that I'm going to make him an offer he can't refuse?' First off, I was like, who is Marlon Brando? I guessed and said *Step Up*. Then I was asked who painted the ceiling of the Sistine Chapel."

"You knew that one, didn't you?" Keysha asked.

"Michelangelo, right?" I looked at her to confirm my answer.

"Yep," Keysha agreed.

"Anyway, I don't remember what the other question was. I was just happy to get off the stage," I joked as we exited the building.

"Hey, guys, wait," I heard a voice shout from behind us. Once again it was Misalo and Wesley running to catch up. When I looked at Misalo, I noticed that he was limping. I assumed it was due to the injury he'd mentioned.

"Why didn't you guys wait?" asked Wesley.

"I was ready to go," I answered.

"Do you want to know how I did?" Misalo asked.

"He was a beast up there," Wesley spoke for him. "He was asked questions about American sports."

"Oh," I said, not all that impressed.

"Do you guys want to hang out?" Misalo eagerly asked.

"No. I've got to get home."

"Yeah, so do I," said Keysha.

"Besides, the month of September is almost over, and the temperature has begun to turn cooler. I'd end up complaining about how cold it is if we just hung out at a park or something," I said, rubbing my arms, which had goose bumps from a drafty breeze coming from an open door behind me.

"Wesley?" Misalo looked at him, but was clearly disappointed that I had refused to hang out with him.

"Sure. Do you want to grab some pizza?" Wesley asked Misalo.

"Sounds like a plan to me," said Misalo. They said good-bye and walked in the opposite direction. Keysha and I continued on.

eighteen

VIVIANA

LaShaunda and I walked out of the building after tryouts and got onto one of the afternoon school buses. I followed her all the way to the rear of the bus. We sat in the last row. She was nearest to the window, and I sat directly beside her. LaShaunda invited me back to her place because she wanted to show me photographs of her friends in Milwaukee.

"So what's up with you?" LaShaunda asked as she eyed me peculiarly.

"What are you talking about?" I asked, feeling a sudden urge to blow my nose. I searched my purse for some tissue.

"Something about you doesn't fit. You're a hood chick who is a pickpocket that knows how to fight, yet you're a closet nerd?" LaShaunda scratched the crown of her head as if she were truly perplexed.

"I'm not a nerd," I immediately corrected her. I didn't like the stigma that came with the name.

"Then how did you know the answers to the questions being asked? Only a geek would know stuff like that," she pointed out.

Getting defensive I said, "I only did it to irritate my cousin. My answers were probably all wrong."

"I don't know. To me it sounded as if you knew what you were talking about," she said, not believing my explanation.

I tossed out a knee-jerk response. "I read stuff on the internet." I preferred to downplay my intelligence, especially around her.

"I read stuff, too, but it's not like I remember any of it. I don't see how you hold information in your head the way you do," she explained.

"It's not that hard. You can do it." I don't know why, but I changed my tone to an encouraging one.

"I don't need a bunch of useless and random thoughts floating around in my head. I like to keep my mind clear." LaShaunda paused. "I'll bet you are the type of chick that secretly hangs out at a library."

"My old neighborhood library was in gang territory. If I had crossed the line, I would have been jumped. So, no, I don't secretly hang out at libraries. The most I did was hang out on the lakefront. I liked walking along the shoreline barefoot." What I said was only a half truth. When my dad was alive, I could not go to the library because it was in an unsafe area. However, I did like going to the library with my grandmother.

"The hood is like that. In Milwaukee the convenience store where I got food from was in another gang's territory. Going out for food was never fun," LaShaunda said.

"Well, that is one thing I am glad we don't have to deal with in this neighborhood," I admitted.

"Yeah. That is nice," LaShaunda agreed.

The school bus dropped us off on Cottage Grove Avenue near Thornridge High School, which was the rival of Thornwood High. We walked another block before reaching the home of her foster parents. It was a redbrick house in the middle of the block. Although it was small, it appeared to be well kept. LaShaunda opened the door and we walked inside. A man was sitting on the sofa. He had a beer bottle wedged between his thighs. He had been watching television on the brown sofa and glanced at us when we entered.

"This is my friend." LaShaunda pointed at me with her thumb. "We will only be here a minute," she explained to the man. The scruffy-looking man glared at us lustfully. I immediately felt as if a million spiders were crawling on my skin. I got goose bumps when the creepy image formed in my mind. He was stocky, had brown skin, a receding hairline and evil eyes.

"I don't mind being in the house with two pretty women," said the man. He took a long gulp of his beer, but never took his gaze off us.

"Come on," LaShaunda said. I followed her into the small kitchen. There was a door on the right just past the archway. She opened it, and I saw that it led into the basement.

"Is your room down there?" I asked.

"Yeah," she answered, hustling down the steep stairs. Her bedroom was situated along a narrow corridor on the opposite side of the laundry room. In her room was an antique bed and dresser. There was a closet that didn't have a door and a black suitcase along the back wall.

"Have a seat on my bed," LaShaunda said. The bed sat very high and I had to hop onto it. The bed bounced and squeaked as I positioned myself. She went over to the dresser and removed a few photos that were there. She then came and sat opposite me. "This is T.J., my boo." She showed me a photo of her with her arm looped around a thin guy. He had on blue jean shorts, an oversize white T-shirt with an image of an Egyptian pyramid and a baseball cap with the bib turned toward the back.

"Where was this taken?" I asked, noticing bottles of alcohol on a table in the background.

"At a party," she answered.

"How old is T.J.?" I noticed the fullness of his facial hair.

"Nineteen," she said, setting the photo aside. "This is my girl, Bebe." She showed me another photo. Bebe was standing with a group of girls who were lined up in a photo.

"That's her." LaShaunda pointed her out. Bebe had long stringy blond hair, blue eyes and fat cheeks. She was wearing pink pajama pants with a brown short-sleeve top.

"Who are the other girls?"

"Friends," LaShaunda said. She showed me one final photo. It was of a brick building.

"This is where my crew is living at now. T.J. sent this to me a few days ago. This is where I am going, and I want you to come. We wouldn't have to worry about anything. No teachers, no parents and no one telling us what to do."

"Are you girls all right?" A voice startled me.

"We're fine!" LaShaunda snapped at her foster dad. He was standing in the archway between the corridor and her bedroom. It was then that I noticed she didn't have a bedroom door.

"Are you sure? Do you guys want something to drink? A beer maybe?" he asked as I shifted uncomfortably.

"Damn fool. I said we are fine," LaShaunda spoke more forcefully. I suddenly felt my heart jump in my throat.

"Do you have a boyfriend?" her foster dad asked me.

"Yeah," I lied.

"Why are you down here?" LaShaunda was now incensed.

"I live here. This is my house. I can go anywhere I want to in it!" he roared back like a lion.

"Come on, Viviana. Let's go." LaShaunda put her photos away and moved toward the exit. Her foster dad didn't budge.

"What's the password?" he asked, using his body to block her.

"I don't have time to play games with you, man!" LaShaunda's expression toughened.

"This isn't a game. Now what's the password?" he asked again as he belched. The foul scent of his breath lingered, like smoke after a fireworks show.

"Would you move, please?" LaShaunda asked with an upside-down face.

"See. There you go. That's all you had to say. Do you want to give me a hug?" He spread his arms so she could step into his embrace, but she didn't. I gathered from his behavior that he imposed his will on LaShaunda whenever the mood hit him.

"What about you? Can I get a hug from you?" he asked me.

"No," I said and hastily rushed past him. He reached out to touch my hair, but I ducked away from his hand.

Once outside, LaShaunda began venting her anger.

"I can't stand that man!" she shouted out.

"Why is he like that?" I asked as we moved farther away from the house.

"He's crazy. He took all the doors out of my room. I have no privacy. Sometimes at night I catch him standing in my doorway watching me sleep."

"Eww!" I cringed at the thought.

"That's why I sleep with a knife. If he touches me, I

swear I am going to put him in a hospital." LaShaunda slit her throat with her index finger, gesturing what she would do if she were ever touched.

"I don't blame you. Dude is definitely weird. Have you said anything to your foster mom?" I asked.

"What the hell is she going to do?" LaShaunda exploded with unbridled emotion. "If she had to make a choice between her man and me, who do you think she would pick?"

"My mother picked her boyfriend over me. I know how horrible that feels," I said as my mind drifted back to the last time I saw my mother. She had come to visit me with her boyfriend, Martin. Well, actually she had come to see my aunt to borrow money. When she didn't get what she wanted, she left and didn't take me with her. She said she would send for me once she got settled, but that was a while ago.

"So what's the deal with all the stuff you lifted? When are we going to turn it in and get the money for that merchandise?" she asked, switching subjects. I snapped out of my daydream.

"We have to go into the city to get rid of it. I know this guy that my father used to work with. He is a shady pawn shop owner. He's not going to ask us to fill out any forms," I said.

"How much business did your dad do with this guy? Are you sure he isn't going to call the cops on us?" LaShaunda asked.

"I'm positive. My dad told me that people would rent electronics from furniture rental places, then bring them to this pawn shop guy for cash."

"Didn't the rental people come for their stuff?" LaShaunda asked.

"I'm sure they did, but lots of times people used fake information when they rented. I also heard that since the stuff was insured, the rental company would just put in a claim and get the items replaced."

"That's slick," LaShaunda said.

"I know. I'm going to give the guy a call to let him know when we'll be coming through. Then we'll take half of the stuff to him right now," I said. "We'll wait a little while before we pawn the rest."

"Cool." LaShaunda seemed happy. "How much do you think we'll get?"

"We should get a least a few hundred for the iPad and cell phones I lifted. I'm not too sure about the jewelry," I said.

"Whatever we get, it will be more than what we have now," LaShaunda pointed out.

"True." We continued walking. "So what do you want to do now?"

"I don't care, as long as I don't havc to sit in the house with that fool," LaShaunda said.

nineteen

MAYA

Keysha and I walked into the school and took a seat on one of the concrete benches in the noisy commons area. I had to tie my shoelace before I stumbled and fell on my face. There were other students sitting around chatting and waiting for security to tell them it was time to head to class.

"Hurry up. I want to find out if I made the team." Keysha sighed impatiently.

"Jeez, is it that serious?" I asked.

"Yes," Keysha said. Once my shoe was tied, we headed down the corridor in the direction of the auditorium. As we approached, we saw a white sheet of paper taped to the auditorium door.

"It looks as if the team members have been posted," I said. Keysha and I walked up and looked at the names. Keysha then screamed.

"We made it!" She gave me a giant hug.

"Really? I was picked?" I was completely surprised as I took a closer look. Sure enough, there was my name, third on the list behind Viviana and Keysha.

"How did she make the team?" I pointed to Viviana's name. "This has to be a mistake. Viviana could not have made the team. She missed an entire year of high school.

How is this possible?" I fired off the questions, knowing that Keysha didn't know the answers.

"I don't know, but look at this." Keysha pointed out the last person to make the team.

"Misalo!" I blurted out.

"Yes. The team is Viviana, you, Misalo and me," Keysha said.

"I have to go and look out of a window. I swear, pigs must be flying or something if Viviana made the team. We'll never win a single competition with her as a teammate."

"It might not be so bad," Keysha suggested.

"Yes, it will. Why does my life suck so much?" I grumbled as I walked away.

Before long the month of October had arrived. The one thing I loved about October was homecoming. My mom, Anna and I got to spend time shopping for dresses, shoes and other accessories. I loathed the fact that Viviana had to tag along with us because my mother felt obligated to purchase clothing for her, as well. I was actually glad that Anna had come along when we went shopping because she kept Viviana company.

On Saturday I was in my room going through my closet in search of a cute outfit to wear. The homecoming parade was scheduled to take place in an hour. Since the parade marched directly in front of Keysha's house, we decided to show our school spirit by cheering on our football team, cheerleaders and other clubs associated with the weekend festivities. Later, we planned to attend the football game, which was against our rival school, Thornridge, and finally during the evening we'd attend the homecoming dance.

Once I decided on an outfit, I showered, got dressed

and put on a little makeup. I walked into the kitchen and saw my parents sitting at the kitchen table drinking coffee and chatting.

"I'm heading over to Keysha's house to watch the home-coming parade," I said as I moved past them.

"What time will you be back?" asked my father.

"I should only be gone for about an hour," I said.

"Viviana isn't going with you?" asked my mother. I wanted to say, "The only place Viviana needs to go is to hell," but I knew that would not be tolerated.

"No. She has made a friend named LaShaunda. She'll probably go with her. That is, if she has plans to go. I'm not sure if Viviana likes Thornwood enough to show some school spirit," I mentioned as I pulled the patio door open.

"I'm sure she likes Thornwood High. She told me that she made the trivia team. I talked your mother into allowing her to try out because I figured it would give her something constructive to do," said my father. I had forgotten how he and Viviana had bonded because she has a love of history just like he does.

"Oh, yeah, that's right," I said, stepping outside.

"Isn't she on the team with you?" I heard my father ask. Instead of answering him, I waved goodbye and acted as if I didn't hear his question.

When I arrived at Keysha's house, there were several empty chairs already situated on the sidewalk. I walked down her long driveway toward the door.

"I'll be right down," I heard Keysha's voice shout out. I glanced in the direction of her voice and searched for her.

"Up here. I'm in the window," she said.

"Oh. I see you now." I waved.

"Just have a seat. I am on my way now." She pointed toward the chairs on the sidewalk.

I walked back to the seats and sat down. I noticed the street had already been shut down to traffic. A number of Keysha's neighbors had staked out a viewing spot and were waiting patiently for the parade to begin.

"It was warmer than I thought," Keysha mentioned breathlessly as she sat beside me. "I had to go back inside and change clothes."

"I hate October weather. It's hard to know when it is going to be mild or downright cold," I complained.

"We don't have too many more mild days left this year, that's for sure," Keysha mentioned as she glanced at her watch. "It's almost noon. The parade should start at any moment."

"So what are you wearing to the homecoming dance tonight?" I asked.

"A black strapless dress that Grandmother Katie brought for me. I also have some really cute shoes to go with it. When the parade is over, I want you to come up to my room so you can see it," Keysha said, peering down the street.

"Okay. I have a red dress that I'm wearing," I mentioned as I tucked my hair behind my ear.

"Has the parade begun yet?" I heard a gruff voice approaching from behind. It was Keysha's grandmother.

"I think so," Keysha answered. I rose from my seat and greeted Grandmother Katie with a hug. I inhaled her sweet scent and immediately felt her warm spirit.

"How have you been, honey?" she asked as she planted a kiss on my cheek.

"Good," I answered. Grandmother Katie sat with us.

"I really enjoy parades. It reminds me of when I was a

little girl. I used to sit on my father's shoulders and wave at everyone." Grandmother Katie laughed.

The rest of Keysha's family came out of the house—her father, Jordan, and her mother, Barbara. Before long, the parade slowly crept past us. Mike marched by with the football team and did a goofy dance to get Grandmother Katie's attention. She laughed at his silliness. Keysha and I saw several people from school that we knew. We couldn't help but rush over and give them hugs as they continued along the parade route. Once the parade was over, I helped Keysha and her grandmother take the chairs back to the garage and then went up to Keysha's room to see her dress.

A while later, Keysha and I were at the football game. We watched her brother, Mike, score a touchdown on one play and drop the ball during another. The game was close and was won by the rival school, which was able to score a field goal the last few seconds of the game.

I hated going to homecoming alone, but there was nothing I could do about that. I walked into the school, paid for my ticket and headed toward the sounds of music and shouting. The dance was held in the cafeteria. When I entered, the lights had been dimmed, but I could tell that the student council had festooned the cafeteria with banners and balloons. The theme this year was Tonight's Dream, Tomorrow's Memory. There was a makeshift stage set up for the crowning of the homecoming king and queen. The DJ was spinning a popular song and my classmates were gyrating to it with wild abandon. I moved through the crowd toward the concession stand, where I planned to purchase something to drink.

"What can I get for you?" asked Miss Bingham, who had apparently volunteered to work the stand.

"Water, please," I said as I opened my small purse that matched my dress and pulled out some money. Once I paid Miss Bingham, I searched for Keysha. I spotted her on the dance floor with Wesley. They looked very happy and couldn't seem to stop smiling at each other. I decided that it wasn't a good time to interrupt them. I glanced around the cafeteria and spotted Viviana and her friend, LaShaunda. Viviana was wearing the blue-and-black spaghetti-strap dress and high-heeled shoes my mother had purchased for her.

LaShaunda looked as if she had just rolled out of bed. She had on blue jeans and a T-shirt, which made me wonder why her mother hadn't purchased a nice dress for her.

"You look beautiful."

I screamed and then flinched.

"I'm sorry. I didn't mean to startle you."

"Why did you sneak up on me like that, Misalo?" I said, punching his left shoulder.

"I wasn't trying to sneak up on you." He laughed.

"You could have fooled me," I said, jabbing him with my index finger.

"Stop poking me." He smiled. I took a moment to look at him. He was dressed handsomely. He had on nice black slacks with a navy blue shirt and matching vest.

"You look pretty nice yourself," I admitted.

"How long have you been here?" He leaned into me and spoke purposely in my ear so I could hear his words clearly over the music. His warm breath tickled my neck and gave me goose bumps.

"I just arrived," I said, rubbing my bare arms.

"Are you cold? If so, I left my jacket in the car. I could go get it, if you'd like."

"No, I'm fine," I said, looking back in the vicinity where I'd seen Viviana.

"So why aren't you with your new girlfriend?" I asked, just to irritate him.

"I don't have a girlfriend, Maya," Misalo spoke softly.

"Viviana would probably love it if you were to go over and talk to her," I said, pointing in the direction I'd last seen her.

"Will you ever forgive me for being such an idiot?" he asked earnestly. I answered by shrugging my shoulders.

"Maya, I was a jackass. Viviana convinced me that the lies she told were the truth. She should go into politics or something. I am sorry for hurting you so badly." Misalo maneuvered so that he was standing directly in front of me. I studied his somber eyes and saw deep sorrow in them.

"I was blinded by anger and—" he paused for a moment before he whispered "—horniness." His shoulders slumped forward. "When I realized I had lost the most precious person in my life, I mentally beat myself up. In fact, I'm still beating myself up."

"As you should," I said.

"You're right. I just came over to tell you how nice you look. I will leave you alone now," he said and began backing away from me.

Just before he turned his back to me, I blurted out, "Aren't you going to ask me for a dance?"

Misalo paused. He looked as if he wasn't sure he had heard me correctly.

"What did you just say?" he asked, stepping back toward me.

"It would be nice if you asked me for a dance. I like this song," I said. Misalo paid attention to the melody.

"It's a slow song," he said.

"Yeah, I know." I smiled at him. My icy attitude toward him had begun melting. Misalo took my hand and pulled me out to the dance area. Once he found a spot for us, I stepped into his embrace, and we rocked back and forth.

twenty

VIVIANA

when I saw Misalo dancing with Maya, my stomach flipped. I was actually hoping that we would speak to each other. I knew that I wasn't his favorite person, but that didn't mean that he had to ignore me.

"Do you want to get his attention?" LaShaunda asked when she noticed how upset I had become.

"How am I going to do that? He's all hugged up with her," I said.

"We could go and push her out of the way. You stand in front of him and I'll stand behind him. We'll turn him into a sandwich. He's a guy, so he'll like that. It will make him feel special," LaShaunda said.

"No. I don't want to do that," I answered, trying to do a better job of concealing my bruised heart.

"Are you sure? I'm telling you it will work, and if your cousin tries to start a fight, you know that I've got your back."

"If I start a fight with her, Keysha will jump in and she'll fight," I said, shifting uneasily.

"There are plenty of other guys around," LaShaunda pointed out.

"Yeah, but none of them are as special as Misalo." I sighed in frustration as a song called "Stanky Leg" began to play.

"Look, it's my responsibility as your friend to cheer you up and make sure you have fun here tonight. So I'm going to make you laugh by doing the Stanky Leg."

I cracked up at her rendition of the dance. She moved in the goofiest way. "That song and dance is old," I said to her.

"I don't care," LaShaunda said as she squatted down and kicked one leg out to the side.

"You're doing it wrong," I said, laughing and joining in.

As the evening continued, LaShaunda and I danced and gyrated and screamed when the DJ played a popular song that we liked. At one point Red, the boy from my history class, asked if he could dance with me. As he and I danced to a fast-paced song, LaShaunda sandwiched him between us. The grin that spread across Red's face was priceless. I am certain he felt like the ultimate playboy. After the song ended, Red stuck to me and LaShaunda like an insect glued to a strip of flypaper.

About an hour later the music stopped, and one of the teachers began making announcements. He made a comment about the great effort the football team put in even though they didn't win. He held up someone's lost cell phone until a female student stepped forward to claim it. Then the Homecoming King and Queen were announced. The winners were people that neither LaShaunda nor I had ever met or heard of.

"I could have been Homecoming Queen if I wanted to," LaShaunda boasted.

"Why didn't you run?" I asked, encouraging her to continue with the lie she was telling.

"These people aren't ready for me. They're not ready to deal with a true queen," LaShaunda bragged about herself.

"Well, I'm glad you spared everyone, your Royal Highness," said Red, who was standing nearby and overheard LaShaunda.

"Dude, get lost before I punch you in the eye," LaShaunda said. Red laughed and did not take her threat seriously. Another song came on and I began dancing. Red joined me and, for the first time, I realized that I was actually having fun.

That following Monday, the dismissal bell had rung, and the hallway was filled with noisy students leaving for the day. I stood in front of my locker, fumbling with my combination lock, which was jammed. On my third attempt, it finally opened. I placed a few books on the top shelf then squatted down and removed my history and English books. I heard a loud bang from someone slapping the palm of their hand against the locker next to me.

"What's up?" LaShaunda had appeared out of nowhere.

"Nothing," I answered, rising. "I'm on my way to my trivia quiz show practice."

"What is up with you?" asked LaShaunda, irritated.

"What are you talking about?" I asked defensively.

"We have to go and handle some business, and you're worried about some stupid trivia practice?" LaShaunda asked as I noticed one of her eyebrows shoot up.

I didn't relish getting into an argument, but I wanted to go to practice first. "Relax. It will not take that long."

"It's going to take long enough," LaShaunda complained.

"No, it will not," I answered sharply.

"Something is wrong with you. I think you actually

like hanging around with those boring brainy people."
LaShaunda stabbed me in the shoulder a few times with
her finger. I swatted it away once I slammed my locker shut.

"This isn't about hanging out with nerds," I said and
began walking.

LaShaunda popped her fingers then smirked. "Then it
must be about *dude*. You still have a thing for him, don't
you?"

I said nothing and allowed her to draw her own conclu-
sion as she raced to catch up with me.

"Are you trying to hook back up with Misalo?" she asked.

"Thought had crossed my mind. We used to have something very special," I said as I headed to practice.

"So why did dude break up with you?" LaShaunda asked.

"Look. I don't want to talk about it, okay," I said as I
pulled open the door to the auditorium.

"I didn't realize it was such a sensitive subject." She held
her hands up as if she were surrendering to the police.

"Are you coming in or are you going to wait out here?"
I asked.

"Yeah, I'll come in and watch you play with the geek
squad." She laughed condescendingly.

Mr. Morgan had me sit in the front row along with Maya,
Keysha and Misalo. He went over the rules of the game
and how points were earned. He talked about the various
subject areas we needed to become familiar with, as well.

"This is going to require a lot of studying on your part,"
he explained as he reached into a box that was sitting on
top of a table near where he was standing. He removed four
large envelopes.

"What's that?" Maya asked.

"Study materials," Mr. Morgan explained.

"Aw, man, I have to memorize all of this stuff?" Misalo whined.

"It's not about memorizing," Mr. Morgan said as he handed out the packets.

"Do any of you know what the best way to learn is?" he asked.

"Through memorization," Maya said, absolutely certain her answer was correct.

"No," said Mr. Morgan.

"Well, I don't know if this is correct, but I do what my father told me to do. He said that I should not try to memorize anything, but take in information as new knowledge that I can use."

"Bingo." Mr. Morgan pointed at me. "Your father is a very smart man. I am going to show you how to take in and retain knowledge differently. That's one of the secrets to winning. We have a lot of work to do. Today I want to go over what is in the packet, assign some reading and do a game show run-through. So let's get to it. Open up your packets and pull out the study guide."

Mr. Morgan had us practice for two hours. He drilled us on questions, made us read and did various exercises to help us retain information. After LaShaunda saw that I wouldn't be leaving as soon as I had thought, she walked out. I could tell by the cynical expression on her face that she was not happy.

twenty-one

MAYA

SINCE our trivia team was so small, we had to travel on a short yellow bus. I hated riding on the smaller bus. It was too cramped, and the seats were not as comfortable as the ones on the larger buses. The team and I were heading to Homewood High School for our first competition. Students from Thornridge and Hillcrest High would also be there competing. I was both nervous and excited at the same time. I silently quizzed myself, but it only added to my sense of anxiousness. I felt as if my brain had locked up. I shifted myself to look at Misalo, who was sitting at the back of the bus with his earbuds in. He was bobbing his head to the beat of some song while he stared out the window. He had told me that it was his way of focusing before competitions.

"Augh!" I complained loudly.

"Are you okay?" asked Keysha, who was sitting in the seat across the aisle from me, toying with her cell phone.

"This bus has the worst shocks. I feel like I'm a ball being bounced." I exhaled as I smashed my head into the seat back.

"It's not that bad," Keysha said.

"It's bad enough." I glanced at Keysha, and she nodded her head in the direction of Viviana, who was sitting in front of us behind the bus driver and across the aisle from Mr. Morgan.

"What's wrong with her? Why is she so quiet?" Keysha whispered.

"I think her friend is mad at her."

"Oh," said Keysha, distracted by a video clip she was watching on her cell phone.

"Why ask me a question and then tune me out?" I didn't like how rude Keysha was being by allowing her cell phone to be a distraction.

"Girl, would you just relax? You're all wound up," Keysha said.

"I'm trying to, but my mind will not stop racing," I reluctantly admitted.

"You'll be fine." Keysha continued to scroll through her phone. "Oh, wow. Look at this. I just came across something I had totally forgotten about," she whispered and then waved for me to come and sit directly beside her.

"What kind of video is it?" I leaned closer to her.

"Shhh. Just look," Keysha said as if she were about to show me a disgusting video.

"What the hell," I said out loud. Keysha jabbed me with her elbow.

"Be quiet. I don't want Mr. Morgan to come back here."

"Is that?" I pointed to the back of Viviana's head.

"Yes," Keysha said. "I shot it when Wesley and I were at Lollapalooza."

I cupped my hand and placed it against Keysha's ear and whispered, "It looks like she's pickpocketing."

Keysha nodded her head and confirmed that I was right.

"Can you email that to me? It might come in handy," I said.

"Sure. I meant to show it to you a while back, but I forgot." Keysha attached the video clip to an email and sent it.

A short while later we parked at Homewood High School, got off the bus and walked into the auditorium. There were more people there than I had anticipated. The audience not only consisted of the other teams, but of parents and teachers. There must have been at least fifty people who had come out to watch. The stage had two sets of game show podiums where four players each from two schools could stand and one podium for the moderator. Whatever school won the first round would have to go up against the winner of the second round. The losing schools would then compete against each other for second place. After checking in and getting settled, I learned that we were up first and had to compete against Thornridge High School.

We walked onto the stage and took our spot at the game show podium. Viviana was in the first position, Keysha was in the second, I was in the third and Misalo was in the fourth.

"Are you ready to do this, babe?" asked Misalo, who had reached over and placed his hand on top of mine.

"I'm nervous and my hands are cold," I whispered to him.

"You'll be fine," he tried to assure me.

The moderator introduced herself as Jane, the librarian from Homewood. She had a very soothing voice, a pleasant smile and wore glasses. She gave us instructions and told us that we had to press a buzzer in order to answer the questions. The button trigger was very sensitive and would determine who pressed it first. Another librarian from Homewood High named Kathy was the scorekeeper. Kathy waved to all the contestants with a warm smile that made me feel a little more at ease.

"Are you ready for this?" I leaned over and asked Keysha. She tapped her index finger like a telegraph operator against the surface of the game show podium.

"Yeah. I just want to get the show on the road," she said as she bit down on her bottom lip. I looked a little farther down at Viviana. She had a solemn expression on her face that was difficult for me to interpret. I couldn't tell if she was concentrating or had completely freaked out. She had totally zoned out, which I thought was weird.

"Okay. Thornridge High, are you ready?" asked Jane. The Thornridge High players said yes.

"Thornwood players, are you ready?" she asked us, and we all said yes.

Jane read the first question. "The industrial revolution began in the late eighteenth century in what country?" I heard a quick ding and realized a Thornridge High player wanted to answer.

"The United Kingdom," answered a girl with fiery red hair and freckles.

"That is correct," said Jane. "Most major earthquakes occur along the rim of what ocean?" Again, there was another ding indicating that a Thornridge player had pressed the button first and had an answer.

"The Pacific Ocean," answered a scrawny-looking guy with chapped lips.

"That is correct," answered Jane.

"We're getting our butts kicked," I mumbled.

"*Getting Played* is a novel written by what American author?"

Keysha pressed the buzzer first this time. "Celeste Norfleet," she answered.

"That is correct," said Jane.

"Yes." Keysha pumped her fist.

"What is the oldest major baseball park still in use?" asked Jane.

Misalo hit the buzzer first that time. "Fenway Park," he answered.

"That is correct," said Jane.

I reached over and touched Misalo's hand briefly.

"Pablo Picasso, Alexander Graham Bell and General Patton all had what common reading disorder?" asked Jane, but no one pressed the buzzer. There was an eerie moment of silence. Finally, Viviana pressed the buzzer.

"Oh, God. I hope she doesn't mess up," I said to myself.

"Dyslexia."

"That is correct," said Jane.

"After twenty days, a frog embryo develops into what fishlike creature?"

I hit the buzzer first on that one. "A tadpole," I answered.

"That is correct," said Jane.

"What 2010 film about stuttering won an Oscar?" asked Jane.

A Thornridge player hit the button first. *"Black Swan,"* the girl with red hair answered.

"No, that is incorrect," said Jane.

Keysha hit the buzzer. *"The King's Speech."*

"Yes, that is correct," said Jane.

"Math question. What is the greatest common factor of twenty and sixteen?" Jane asked.

Viviana hit the buzzer first. "Four," answered Viviana.

"That is correct. What was founded in 1732 as the last of the original thirteen colonies?"

Viviana hit the buzzer. "Georgia."

"That is correct. With over one million participants, what is the most popular sport played in U.S. high schools?"

Misalo hit the buzzer. "Football," he answered.

"That is correct. What river in the Middle East has the lowest elevation in the world?" asked Jane, and again there was pure silence. No one hit the buzzer.

Finally the kid with the chapped lips took a shot. "The Nile?"

"No, that is incorrect. Thornwood, would you like to take a shot at it?"

Keysha decided to press the button. "I am going to guess my dad's name, which is *Jordan,*" said Keysha.

"You've guessed correctly," said Jane.

Keysha released a big sigh.

We gave Thornridge a serious beat down. Our entire team had answered questions correctly. We didn't get any of them wrong. The next competition was won by Homewood High. We battled them and thought for sure we would win easily, but that wasn't the case. The questions got harder, and we began to miss a lot of them. We had run out of time and had to go into a head-to-head round to determine the winner. Keysha wanted to represent us, but Mr. Morgan said that Viviana should do it. The round consisted of one player from each team. They had two minutes to answer a series of questions. Correct answers were worth ten points. However, if you got the answer wrong, ten points were deducted. Viviana was going against a guy who looked like a young Albert Einstein. They walked over to another podium that was carted onto the stage. Each player stood in front of each other with a buzzer in their hand. Jane stood between them with the questions.

"The equator is represented by what degree of latitude?"

Einstein buzzed first. "Zero," he answered.

"Correct," answered Jane. "What city is named the Crescent City and the Big Easy?"

Viviana buzzed first. "New Orleans," she answered.

"Correct," answered Jane.

I thought for sure the competition would be tight, but Viviana blew the guy completely out of the water and answered ten questions in a row correctly. To my utter surprise, we had won our first competition, and it felt great.

twenty–two

Mr. Morgan rushed onto the stage and gave me a giant hug. He was more hyped up than Maya, Misalo, Keysha and I combined. I was happy to see that he was proud of what had been accomplished. The moment caused me to reflect on my father. I know that he would have been just as proud of me. He would have hugged me or given me a high five. My father was so smart and wonderful that I know he would have helped me learn the material. Since my father wasn't around to celebrate my moment of achievement, the feeling of wanting to be acknowledged did not disappear. I wanted to commemorate the victory of winning with someone special. I wanted to celebrate with Misalo. I wanted him to notice that I was just as smart as, if not smarter, than Maya. Deep in my heart I wanted him to give me another chance. As hard as I had tried to let him go, I had not been able to.

At the end of the competition, we shook hands as an expression of sportsmanship with the players from the other schools. Once Misalo had finished shaking everyone's hand, he approached me to give me a handshake.

"Great job, Viviana," he said with his inviting smile that I had become very fond of. I quickly scanned around to see where Maya was. Her back was turned because she and Keysha were still shaking hands with the others. I took that moment to be bold and daring. Instead of giving Misalo a handshake, I gave him a hug and smacked his behind.

"You did pretty good, as well. Call me," I whispered in his ear and kissed his earlobe. Before I could release him, Maya had come over and separated us.

"What the hell, Viviana! You need to back up off of him." She jabbed her bony finger at me as if it were a knife. I laughed at her and walked away.

"At least now Misalo knows that I am not ready for him to be done with me," I muttered to myself as I walked out and headed toward our school bus.

During the bus ride back home, Keysha, Misalo and Maya refused to sit near me. They all sat at the rear of the bus. I knew they were gossiping about me, but I didn't care. I decided to pass the time by looking over some additional material that Mr. Morgan had given to me.

"You were amazing, Viviana," said Mr. Morgan.

"It was nothing." I downplayed the moment. I briefly thought about LaShaunda and how mad she had gotten when I had told her that I wasn't going to the pawn shop with her today. I wasn't in the mood for traveling all the way to the city. I wanted to go to the competition and find out for myself how well I could do.

"It takes a unique mind to be able to retain and recall all the knowledge you've learned," he continued as the bus made a turn too sharply and rolled over a curb.

"I have always been a *Jeopardy!* junkie. Don't ask me why I'm attracted to that show because I don't even know."

"It's probably because you're a genius and don't realize it," he said.

"What?" I laughed at him.

"I'm serious. I think you're very smart, but you don't like people to know it," he said.

"Trust me, Mr. Morgan. I am not a genius. I am not a rocket scientist or an inventor."

"Viviana, a genius is someone embodying exceptional intellectual ability, creativity or originality. I think your intellectual abilities are well developed for a person your age," he said.

I laughed. "You have me confused with someone else."

"I don't think so. I feel that, with the right coaching and development of you and the rest of the team, we could make it to nationals and have a real shot at the championship."

I looked into Mr. Morgan's eyes and saw that he meant every word he had said.

"I am not that good," I said, refusing to accept the notion that I was that excellent at anything.

"Viviana, you have to stop doubting yourself. Young lady, you can become a leader. You could lead this team if you would only step up and show a little leadership." He beamed with pride and for some reason that I cannot explain, Mr. Morgan's passionate words caused my heart to sink into the pit of my belly. I couldn't tell if I was feeling fear or dread or a combination of both.

"I want you to seriously think about stepping up and leading the team," he said.

"They don't even like me, Mr. Morgan," I whispered.

"They don't have to like you, but they will have to learn to respect you. If you can get them to like and respect you, then you would have done something that most students in your situation would not have even attempted. I think that is the type of challenge you should take on."

I looked back at the three of them huddled at the rear of the bus and sighed.

"Go on and enjoy the victory with them," Mr. Morgan encouraged me. I was about to give it a shot when my cell phone buzzed. I had just received a text message from my younger cousin, Anna. She said that her parents had found a backpack filled with electronics and jewelry. They had been drilling Anna and her brother about it, and I should be ready for the inquisition because her mom was on a warpath.

"Damn," I hissed.

When I got off the bus, Maya and Keysha got into Misalo's car and drove off. They didn't offer me a ride or even say goodbye. It wasn't like I expected a ride, but I still felt the sting of being outside their clique. The sun had already set and it was dark. I decided to take my time walking home because I knew that I had hell waiting on me when I arrived at the door.

I walked on unsteady legs up the driveway. I had decided that the best thing to do was to deny any knowledge of the stolen items in the bag. I hoped that my aunt Raven would believe me and not accuse me the way she had when Anna had inadvertently overdosed on drugs. I will never forget how I was demonized for something I had not done. I don't do drugs, sell drugs or even knowingly hang around people who do drugs.

Instead of walking in the front door, I decided to go around back and enter through the patio door. Once I stepped inside, I saw my backpack and an assortment of jewelry, cell phones and the iPad I had scored spread out on the mahogany kitchen table. My aunt Raven was sitting at the table. When she looked at me, all I saw was hell in her eyes.

"Have a seat!" Her hand thudded against the table loudly. I knew right then that she was beyond angry.

"That's not my bag or my stuff," I said, feeling more defensive than usual. I took a seat opposite her. A few moments later Uncle Herman walked in and sat next to my aunt Raven.

"Then who does it belong to?" asked my aunt Raven.

"Uhm." I stalled as I searched my mind for a good lie. "LaShaunda."

"Who the hell is LaShaunda?" Uncle Herman asked with a tone of voice that caused me to flinch with fear. His raised voice was not something I was accustomed to.

"A girl at school asked me to hold that bag for her. I never knew what was in it," I continued to lie.

"Is that right?" My aunt Raven thumped her index finger against her temple. She glared at me as if she were a predator and I was her prey.

"Tell the truth, Viviana!" Uncle Herman growled at me.

"I am telling the truth," I gruffly answered, hoping they would believe my lie. I didn't understand why they were not taking my word for it. I decided to try making them feel guilty for accusing me, by playing the role of a victim. "You guys are blaming me for something I had nothing to do with. The same way you blamed me when Anna got sick. Why am I always getting nailed whenever something around here goes wrong?" I gave my uncle Herman a teary-eyed look. I had hoped that I could soften his heart and win his sympathy.

"Maya!" Aunt Raven screamed out her name.

"Yes. Here I come," Maya answered as if even she were

afraid of her mom. She walked into the kitchen. Maya looked at me briefly, and I noticed something in her eyes. She had said or done something to get me in trouble, but I didn't know what, though. I glanced just past Maya and saw Anna wiping tears away from her eyes. That alarmed me.

"What's going on?" I toughened my voice. I felt as if I had been backed into a corner.

"Show her the video clip," said Aunt Raven.

"Video clip? Is this some type of joke?" I said, realizing the seriousness of the situation had gone to another level. Maya pressed a few buttons on her cell phone and then handed it to her mom. Aunt Raven pointed the screen at me and that's when my mouth dropped open and my eyes grew wide with shock. It was a very clear video of me at Lollapalooza pickpocketing some guy's iPhone. I had no idea how Maya got the video.

"I heard the phone beeping when I was out in the shed this afternoon. The owner turned on the locater and sent a text message that said 'I'm going to find you,'" said my uncle Herman.

"Uhm." I choked up.

"He was all set to call the goddamn police and come to the house with them to retrieve his stolen property and press charges!" my aunt Raven screamed at me. "Do you think for one minute that I want the goddamn police at my home! You've disrespected this house for the last time, Viviana! You're a liar and a thief, and I'm not going to put up with you!"

"You're lucky that I was able to text the man back and tell him that it wasn't necessary to get the police involved," Uncle Herman shouted. He was so angry that I could see the cords in his neck tightening up.

I did not want to cry, but I could not help it. Tears streamed down my cheeks.

"Why did you do it, Viviana?" Aunt Raven asked.

"That's what I want to know as well, Viviana. We've shown you nothing but love, compassion and understanding. Why did you do this?" asked Uncle Herman.

I remained silent and focused on the ceiling. I didn't have an answer, and I didn't know what to say. The only thing on my mind at that moment was disappearing. I didn't want to be here. I felt like an outsider and as if I were never truly welcomed. I wanted to be with my mother, but I couldn't because she had abandoned me.

"Answer me, goddamn it!" Aunt Raven sprung to her feet and reached for me. My reflexes were too quick. I had immediately jumped out of my seat and onto my feet. Aunt Raven wanted to beat me. I could see the blinding-white rage in her eyes. Uncle Herman held her back.

"I should have let the police come and lock you up, just like they locked up your father!"

"Don't you talk about my dad!" I pointed my finger at her. My father was off-limits and I would allow no one, not even my aunt Raven, to disrespect my memory of him.

"You've turned out to be just like him. You're a waste of everyone's time and effort. I refuse to live with a liar and a thief!" Aunt Raven's words were as sharp as a surgeon's scalpel and they cut deeply into my emotions.

"Viviana, go to your room. Get out of here. We don't want to see your face right now!" Uncle Herman let go of my aunt. As I walked past her, I could tell that she truly wanted to beat me. I ran up the stairs past Anna and Paul to my bedroom, shut the door and cried.

★ ★ ★

I awoke at midnight to the sound of my cell phone buzzing. My weary eyes were tired from crying and had difficulty focusing. I finally realized that LaShaunda was calling me.

"Hello?" I groggily answered.

"Girl, he had it coming." LaShaunda's voice was distraught and angry.

"What?" I asked, not understanding what she was talking about.

"My foster dad. He had it coming," LaShaunda repeated herself. It was then that I noticed that she was breathing hard. I tossed back the covers and walked into the bathroom because I didn't want to wake Anna.

"What's going on?" I asked cautiously.

"I stabbed him," LaShaunda said.

"You did what?" I asked again to make sure that I heard her correctly.

"He tried to rape me so I stabbed him," LaShaunda spoke more clearly.

"Oh, God. Are you okay?" I asked.

"I am fine. I put a knife right through the center of his hand. You should have heard the way he screamed in pain," LaShaunda said.

"Where was your foster mom?" I asked.

"She was visiting her mother, who is ill. That's why he tried to have his way with me," LaShaunda said angrily.

"Oh, my God! What happened after that?" I asked.

"I quickly tossed what I could in a duffel bag and ran out of the house. I'm going back to Milwaukee to hang with my crew tonight. Are you coming or not?"

I was silent for a moment. "My family hates me," I blurted out as I fought back tears.

"That's nothing new. How long are you going to stay there and let them disrespect you? Huh? How much more of your cousin's BS are you going to take? You're a fool if you stay," LaShaunda said.

"I know," I agreed with her.

"So come with me. Once we hook up with my crew in Milwaukee, we won't have anything to worry about. We look out for each other, and we don't let other people bother us. I've already connected with them, and they said that they have a place for me to stay. I'm sure there is enough room for you, too."

"My uncle found all the stuff I scored, and I got busted," I explained.

"To hell with them, girl. It's time to get real! It's time to make a move," LaShaunda said more forcefully.

"You're right. I'm ready to leave. It's not like my mother is ever coming back for me," I concluded.

"Come on then. Just grab what you need and let's go. Meet me at the Oasis diner that sits above the expressway. We can hitchhike. I'll work on getting one of the truckers sleeping over there to take us."

"I don't want to hitchhike," I said.

"You got a better idea besides walking?" LaShaunda asked.

"I have a little money. I have enough to buy us both a bus ticket and pay for a cab ride downtown to the bus station," I said.

"My girl. I'm glad you got it like that. Meet me at the corner of 147th and Chicago Road. I'll be sitting on the bus bench. You can call for a cab once you get here,"

"Okay," I said.

"Viviana, travel light. Don't bring a suitcase full of stuff," LaShaunda said.

"Okay," I repeated and hung up the phone.

twenty-three

MAYA

I awoke early and showered. Then I got dressed, grabbed my books and rushed out of the house. Keysha and I were meeting up in the library because we both needed to do research for a paper we had to write. The bogus thing about writing the paper was that we could not cite any sources from the internet. We had to use physical books.

By the time I arrived at the school's library, Keysha had already found a seat and waved me over to her.

"Hey. How much time do we have?" I yawned.

"About forty-five minutes," Keysha said, unzipping her backpack and pulling out a folder.

"That's not much time," I said.

"Tell me about it. Studying for that quiz show is no joke. I stay up late going over dates and facts." Keysha sighed.

"That makes two of us," I said.

"Well, at least we won our first competition." Keysha pulled out the instructions she had been given for her research paper.

"Speaking of winning, I have to tell you what happened last night," I said, perking up.

"Let me guess. You had drama with Viviana?" Keysha said sarcastically.

"Well, yes and no," I said.

"What does that mean?" Keysha asked.

I leaned in closer and began to whisper. I didn't want Miss Bingham to come over and tell us that we were being too loud. "When Misalo dropped me off last night, I walked into the house and was grilled by my parents."

"About what? I thought you said this was about Viviana?"

"It is. Just listen. My dad was out in the shed, when he came across a backpack full of cell phones, jewelry and an iPad."

"Why was that there?" Keysha asked with a puzzled look on her face.

"Well, that's what my parents wanted to know," I said.

"They thought it was your stuff?" Keysha caught on quickly.

"Yep. They wanted to know why and how that stuff was at the house. I told them that I had no clue. They had already nailed Anna and Paul, so that meant it must've been Viviana's."

"Oh, snap. That was the stuff she had gotten from pickpocketing people, wasn't it?" Keysha now had the full picture.

"Bingo. So I told my parents about the video you had captured and showed it to them. Sure enough, the iPhone she had snatched was the same one that was beeping."

"Oh, my God. What happened next?" Keysha hung on my every word.

"My parents said that we're going to give Viviana a chance to explain herself. When she got home and was asked about it, she lied and said that it was LaShaunda's."

"She lied to your parents, and they already knew the truth?" Keysha asked for clarification.

"Yep," I answered.

"Dang. She was straight-up busted," Keysha said.

"You should've seen the look on her face when my mother called me into the kitchen where they were. She asked me to pull up the video and then held it so that Viviana could see it."

"She should have just told it like it was. She should have said 'I'm sorry, but, yeah, I stole some stuff,'" Keysha concluded.

"Well, it wasn't like that would have made anything better," I said.

"I know, but still she should have come clean," Keysha said.

"Well, she didn't, and my parents finally saw Viviana for what she truly was. A liar and a thief," I said, full of self-righteousness.

"Did she say why she did it?" Keysha asked.

"Ironically, she decided to mentally check out when that question was asked," I said.

"So what do you think your parents are going to do?" Keysha leaned back and balanced herself on the rear legs of the chair.

"She'll probably get grounded," I said.

"That means she won't be able to compete with the team at tonight's competition." Keysha paused for dramatic effect.

"Wow. I had not thought about that," I said gloomily.

"This sucks. All of that studying has now gone to waste," Keysha complained.

"Maybe not. Perhaps my folks will still allow her to compete," I said, even though I knew the chances of that happening were slim to none.

At the end of the day, Misalo, Keysha and I boarded the

bus heading to our next competition. When Mr. Morgan boarded, he clapped his hands and said, "Are you guys ready to beat the mess out of Thornton High School?" He paused and realized that Viviana wasn't there. "Where is Viviana?"

"I don't know," I said.

"Call her and find out," Mr. Morgan insisted. I loathed the fact that he knew Viviana was my cousin. I pulled out my phone and called her, but I got no answer.

"She's not answering," I said to him.

"Are you serious?" Mr. Morgan exhaled loudly. "I should have known something was wrong when I did not see her in class today."

It was then that I realized that I cared so little for Viviana that I had not noticed her absence. I was positive my parents had grounded her, but not to the point that they would have forced her to stay home and not come to school.

"I'll call my sister. She probably knows where she is," I said and dialed Anna. "Hey. Do you know where Viviana is?" I asked.

"No."

"Well, have you seen her?" I asked.

"Not since last night," Anna answered.

"Have you talked to her at all?" I asked.

"Have you?" Anna snipped. "You're the one who placed the nail in her coffin with the video clip."

"I didn't force her to…" My phone went dead. The little brat had hung up on me. I looked at Mr. Morgan, who was waiting for an answer.

"My sister doesn't know where she is," I said.

"I knew I should've assigned an alternate. Damn." Mr. Morgan was frustrated. "Wait here. I'll be right back."

"What's going on?" Misalo walked from the rear of the

bus to the front where Keysha and I sat. He had been doing his usual pre-competition zone out.

"Viviana is not here," Keysha answered.

"Where is she?" Misalo looked at me.

I shrugged my shoulders. "I don't know where she is."

Ten minutes later Mr. Morgan came walking back toward the bus with Red, one of the students from class.

"Red is going to fill in for us," said Mr. Morgan as he and Red got on the bus.

"What's up, guys," said Red with a giant smile.

"Do you even know how to play?" Keysha asked.

"He isn't going to answer questions. He will be just a body. We will worry about getting him up to speed after this game," said Mr. Morgan.

"Relax, Keysha. I got this," Red said boastfully.

"Great," Misalo said sarcastically and walked to the rear of the bus once more.

We lost the competition, and the bus ride back home was a quiet one. Red did not help matters because he kept pressing the buzzer and giving out the wrong answer, which caused the team to lose points instead of gain them. When we arrived at the school later that evening, Mr. Morgan told us to make sure we were at practice.

"And tell Viviana that I want to see her," he said.

"I will, but she might be grounded," I admitted to him.

"I still want to talk to her. If she's grounded, then we will have to continue on with Red," he said.

Misalo and I dropped Keysha off at home, and then he drove me home. Before I got out of the car, we kissed and hugged each other. It had been a long time since we had kissed, and his lips were still soft and had the power to make me melt.

"Good night," I said then opened the car door.

"Bye," he said. I closed the door and he pulled off.

When I walked into the house, I was surprised to see Grandmother Esmeralda sitting at the kitchen table holding on to her rosary. She had a grim expression on her face, which unsettled me. Anna and Paul were standing next to my mother, who was on the phone.

"Maya, why didn't you answer your phone? I have been calling you for over an hour," my father said.

"Oh. We have to turn our cell phones off when we are competing," I said, reaching in my purse to retrieve it. "What's going on?"

"Honey, have you seen your cousin?" asked my grandmother.

"I saw her last night," I answered.

"Have you seen her since then?" my grandmother asked with an unsteady voice.

"No," I said and then took a seat at the table.

My mother ended her phone conversation and asked, "Do you know where Viviana could possibly be?"

"No, Mom, I don't," I answered. "Why? Is she missing?"

"Yes," my mother said and combed her fingers through her hair. Her eyes were weary and red. "No one has seen her since the argument last night, and the school called to tell me that she had not shown up. She has an honors English class that she will probably fail because of absences. I thought she may have run to your grandmother's, but she had not. I just called all the hospitals in the area, and she's not at any of them."

"I think we should get the police involved," said my father.

"No. Viviana is a good girl. She is just misunderstood. No police. Not yet," Grandmother Esmeralda insisted. "Herman, go drive around. See if she is at the mall or something. Maya, you go with your father. You can help him."

"Fine," said my dad and grabbed his car keys off the countertop.

"Herman," said Grandmother Esmeralda. "I know that getting the police involved is the right thing to do. I just want to give Viviana a chance to come to her senses and call home. I know she will."

"If she doesn't, we will have no other choice but to inform the authorities," my dad said before we walked out the door.

twenty-four

VIVIANA

Lashaunda and I were able to catch a Greyhound bus to Milwaukee the following morning at 6:00 a.m. We arrived in Milwaukee about an hour and a half later. The Greyhound bus station in Milwaukee doubled as the Amtrak train station. The terminal looked fairly new, as if it had recently been built or remodeled. The morning was chilly, but bright and promising. I walked through the terminal with a black duffel bag filled with clothes slung over my shoulder. The terminal was filled with travelers. Some were departing while others were waiting patiently or sleeping in uncomfortable-looking positions.

"I need a shower and to brush my teeth," I said to LaShaunda as I walked beside her.

"Dang, girl, stop your complaining. You can do all that once we get to where we are going," LaShaunda said.

"Tell me about this place where you and your friends stay at again." I kept prying.

"It's like I told you. It's a place where everyone is cool. No one will bother you. You can do whatever you want and it's cool. As long as you're with me, my crew will have your back."

"What about food and clothes? I didn't bring much," I said.

"Girl, please. What do you need clothes for? It's not like you have to go to school. We're done with school. You have now officially graduated. Congratulations." LaShaunda chuckled, but I didn't.

"Will you just relax? It's going to be okay, trust me," she said as we exited the terminal.

"Which way do we go?" I asked, squinting my eyes.

"This way," she said and then pointed. "We have to get to Grand Avenue Mall. That's where the buses are."

"How much does it cost to get on the bus? I only have a few bucks," I said as I readjusted the duffel bag.

"I've never paid to get on the bus. When the damn thing stops and people get off through the rear exit, I jump on. The bus driver doesn't care," LaShaunda said assuredly.

We walked to the corner of West Wisconsin Avenue and Third Street. We stood in front of an Applebee's restaurant, which was next to the entrance to the mall. The area we were in was very clean. I felt comfortable and safe as I watched people heading to work.

"How far is the crew's house from here?" I asked.

"It's on the other side of town. It shouldn't take us that long to get there," LaShaunda said as she sat down on the steps that led to the mall entrance. I dropped my duffel bag and sat beside her. A short time later, the bus arrived.

"Okay, this is us," LaShaunda said as she stood up and grabbed her bag. We walked to the rear of the bus and snuck on as soon as the last passenger got off.

"See. It was a piece of cake." LaShaunda smiled proudly. The bus pulled off and before long, we were on our way.

"So do you think your foster parents are going to look for you?" I asked.

"I don't give a damn what happens to them! They can rot in hell for all I care. The most important thing right now is that I'm free. I can do what I want, when I want and however I want. No rules, no curfews and best of all, no school. Like I told you, the street is my classroom," LaShaunda boasted. "So what happened with you last night?"

"My family hates me, and I'm tired of the BS. Last night was the last straw. I had to show them that I wasn't going to stand around and be disrespected," I said, not owning up to the fact that their anger toward me was justified.

"Well, I know everyone in the crew is going to love you. Just wait, you'll see," LaShaunda said. After what seemed like an eternity, we got off the Wisconsin Avenue bus and caught the Twenty-Seventh Street bus. We finally got off that bus at the corner of West Chambers and North Twenty-Seventh Streets. The area looked isolated. There was a place called Chuck's Smoke Shop, but it was closed, and I had no idea what a smoke shop was.

"Come on. I see the place they told me to come to," LaShaunda said as she trotted across the street toward a white frame house that was nothing like the brick structure she had shown me in the photo. Opposite the house was a vacant lot with overgrown grass and debris, like old car tires, burned-out trash cans and abandoned furniture. LaShaunda walked up the steps toward the front door, which was boarded up.

"Hey!" she shouted out at the top of her voice.

"I don't think anyone lives there. The door is boarded up. Are you sure you have the right address?" I asked, concerned because an abandoned house is not what I had envisioned.

In fact, I had no idea what I envisioned, but I knew that it wasn't the dilapidated house I was standing in front of.

Someone stuck their head out of an upstairs window and yelled, "Who there?" I looked up and saw this girl with scraggly blond hair that looked like it had not seen a comb in years. Her skin was ghostly and dirty, and her eyes reminded me of a fish.

"What's up, girl! It's me, LaShaunda."

"Who that with you? She not the police, is she?" asked the blond-haired girl.

"Come on, Bebe. You know me better than that. This is my friend. She's with me. We came to stay with everybody," LaShaunda said.

"Well, I hope you don't come in here starting trouble." The girl looked at me as if she were evaluating my self-worth.

"Bebe, stop tripping, girl," LaShaunda joked with her.

"Come around the back and I'll let you in."

"Come on, girl," said LaShaunda, who actually had the audacity to be excited about entering the dwelling. We walked around the house and the back door was also boarded up.

"How do we get inside?" I asked as a feeling of dread washed over me.

"Right there, through the small window." LaShaunda pointed to Bebe who was opening the window. LaShaunda squatted down, tossed her bag through the window and crawled inside.

"Are you serious?" I asked.

"Come on. It's okay," LaShaunda tried to assure me. "Don't be like that. This is how we do it." I looked around and saw a pack of stray dogs approaching.

"Damn," I said and crawled inside. It smelled like a combination of mildew and mold on the inside. The moment the foul air entered my lungs, I coughed. The house was eerily silent and dark. Bebe closed the window to ensure that the stray dogs didn't get in. The window I had crawled through placed me in the kitchen. The only sunlight that was able to get through, other than the kitchen window, came from holes in the wood that covered the doors and remaining glass. Lit candles were scattered on the floor. They illuminated some of the darkness, but judging from the rank odor wafting in the air, none of them was scented. The walls had holes and were covered with some type of black residue. If I had to guess, I would say that the dwelling was on fire at some point in time. I glanced above my head and saw exposed pipes that ran from one side of the room to the other. The floor was a combination of old wood and busted tile. There were a few charred kitchen cabinets dangling off the wall above the space where a dated-looking stove stood. I wanted to puke. The smell inside was almost too much to stomach. Then I realized why. To my right there was a small pantry with human waste on the floor.

"Gross," I mumbled and quickly moved past it.

"Is you okay?" Bebe asked.

She used incorrect grammar and talked very slowly as if her brain had to think about the words it was trying to tell her mouth to say.

"She's fine." LaShaunda spoke for me, but I was far from fine.

"It's okay. We family here." Bebe touched my hair and I flinched.

"What are you doing?" I looked at her wide-eyed.

"Yo' hair be so pretty and soft all the time, don't it?"

She smiled and that's when I noticed that several of her teeth were missing. She looked nothing like she had in the photo LaShaunda had shown me. She must have felt self-conscious about it because she quickly stopped smiling and just smirked. I didn't answer her question as I took another step deeper into hell.

"Where is my baby, T.J., at?" LaShaunda asked.

"T.J.? Who is that?" I asked fearfully.

"That's my guy. Remember I told you about him," LaShaunda reminded me, but at that moment I was busy trying to process the environment I had just entered. I was also freaking out because LaShaunda seemed to have transformed into a complete stranger on me. I suddenly realized that I didn't know as much about her as I thought I had.

"Oh," I said, fearing that I had made a huge mistake.

"He's up that hallway. He been waiting on you," said Bebe. I followed LaShaunda down the dank and dark corridor. We entered the front living area, which was illuminated by more candles. Most of the furniture was gone. There was a stale-smelling couch missing its cushions. There were funky-looking mattresses on the floor. On one of them a guy and a girl were sleeping, and on another, there was a guy sticking a needle in his arm.

"Drug addicts," I whispered to myself with a trembling voice.

"T.J. What's up, baby?" LaShaunda called out to her guy who was resting on yet another mattress with his back propped against the wall.

"You finally decided to come back to me."

T.J. had what looked to be dreadlocks and scraggly facial hair. He was very thin and his eyes were set deep in their sockets. LaShaunda kissed him and my stomach did a flip.

I didn't understand how she could possibly feel good about kissing a guy who not only looked dirty, but smelled like he had not showered in months.

"You've put on some weight," said T.J., who was standing on wobbly legs. My intuition told me that he was coming down from a drug high.

"Where is the bathroom?" I politely asked.

"Who is that?" asked T.J., pointing at me.

"She's good people. She treated me nice while I was out in the world trying to live. She's new to this life, but she's ready to be part of the family. She needs to be broken in, though." LaShaunda spoke as if I was suddenly meaningless.

"Broken in? What are you talking about?" I swallowed hard after I asked the question.

"Would you relax, girl. Damn. You're making everybody nervous," LaShaunda scolded me. This was a new side of her personality that I had not seen before. I knew she was jagged around the edges, but not to this extent.

"The bathroom is anywhere you can squat and pee, but most of us use the pantry at the end of the hall," T.J. answered my question.

"What?" I asked, horrified.

"If you don't want to go in there, there is a McDonald's down the street." T.J. offered me another option.

"LaShaunda, can I talk to you for a moment?" I think I was going into shock.

"Chill out, okay? I am going to spend a little time with T.J. Just sit down someplace. No one is going to bother you," LaShaunda insisted.

"Hey, don't nobody mess with this girl," T.J. yelled out. The couple sleeping together didn't move. The guy with the needle in his arm was higher than a satellite in orbit, and Bebe was standing behind me.

"Do you want to do it together?" Bebe whispered in my ear and I jumped. I turned and glared at her.

"I got crack, meth and a little heroin." Bebe continued talking slowly. "I got it for you for a small price."

"Get away from me," I warned her.

"Suit yourself, baby girl. No sweat off my back. Just means more for me." Bebe held up the palms of her hands in a nonthreatening manner. "I was just trying to make you feel at home. Help you take the edge off."

"Viviana, what have you gotten yourself into?" I asked myself as I thought about what to do next.

I crawled back out the window and into the sunlight. I didn't have any money, and I wasn't sure which direction I needed to go to get to someplace that was safe. I reached for my cell phone to call my mother and ask what I should do, but my cell phone was dead. In my hastiness, I hadn't grabbed my charger. It would not have mattered because I doubted if there was electricity in the rotted-out structure LaShaunda had brought me to. I decided to just walk, but stopped and dropped to the ground when I heard gunshots. Someone was driving down the alley opposite me, shooting. I heard someone return fire, but I was too afraid to lift my head. Once the shooting stopped, I crawled backward, found a wall and squatted down on the road. I rested my forehead on my knees and tried to figure out why my life was spiraling out of control.

I decided to go back and force LaShaunda to at least point me in the direction of the bus terminal. I stupidly hadn't paid attention to exactly how I got to the location I was at. I would rather sleep in a bus station than squat in an abandoned building. I rose to my feet and went back toward the boarded-up house. When I got there, I saw that both T.J. and LaShaunda were spaced out. LaShaunda could barely hold her head up.

"LaShaunda." I shook her, but she was incoherent. I placed her face in my hands and looked into her eyes. She was nodding in and out.

"LaShaunda?" I tapped her cheeks rapidly several times. I thought she may have just been in a deep sleep.

"LaShaunda!" I tapped her cheeks again, but her soul was not at home. I scanned the floor around her. That was when I noticed her exposed arm, the needle mark and dried blood just above her forearm. It all suddenly made sense. The blemishes I had noticed on her arm were the result of drug usage. When she asked if I got high, I assumed she meant smoking weed. I had not considered that she meant another type of drug.

"No!" I cried out as I tried to understand why I had missed the warning signs of LaShaunda's addiction. I wanted to cry, but I was in shock and couldn't remember how.

There was no way I was going to sleep. I stayed awake. I don't why I didn't leave. Perhaps a part of me felt sorry and responsible for LaShaunda. When T.J., LaShaunda and the rest of her crew came down from their high, the morning sun had come up. The couple that was asleep on the mattress and the single guy awoke first. They moved past me like three zombies. Neither one said a word to me or each other. They crawled out the window and disappeared. Then T.J. and LaShaunda awoke. LaShaunda was more coherent, but different. Her eyes and behavior were different.

"You've got to try it, girl." LaShaunda was jittery.

"What the hell are you talking about?" I asked, noticing that several candles had burned out.

"T.J. took me to another level yesterday. Heroin is amazing. You would not believe how it makes you feel." LaShaunda spoke as if she'd taken a flight into outer space. "I told T.J. about you and how you know how to pickpocket people. You can steal stuff and take it to the pawn shop up here and get us money so we can do this again and again."

"Have you been on drugs all this time?" I wanted to cry, not out of sadness, but anger.

"Try it. Girl, I'm telling you. You will feel so good," LaShaunda said. It was then that I knew she was no longer my friend, and I had to get out. I backed away from her and bumped into Bebe.

"Where are you going so fast?" Bebe asked.

"I need some air," I said and moved toward the window. The three of them moved along with me.

"We need some air, too," said T.J.

"And some food," said Bebe.

"Let's go hit Family Dollar," T.J. said. "You're coming with us. There will be people there that you can rob."

"She's really good, too, man."

I couldn't believe LaShaunda had offered me to the group as if my feelings and thoughts were meaningless. I wanted to grab my duffel bag, but didn't think it was a good idea since the three of them had forced me to walk past it. I crawled out the window, and my first thought was to run, but I didn't. I felt lost and confused. I had never been in a situation like this. I had never had someone turn on me or set me up like this. The fall air was cold and goose pimples formed on my arms. I hugged myself in an effort to contain my body heat.

"Come on." T.J. grabbed my right arm just above my elbow. Bebe stood on the other side of me and did the same thing.

"LaShaunda." I looked over my shoulder and called to her. I wanted to tell her to get her friends before I beat them down.

"Relax, girl," LaShaunda said and began laughing like a lunatic.

"She told me about your fighting skills. You try anything and I will shoot you down like a dog." T.J. lifted his shirt and showed me the handle of a gun.

"Why are you doing this?" I asked.

"So we can get high. That's the goal for the day and the goal every day. Get money and get high," T.J. explained.

"We're going to walk into Family Dollar, snatch some food and walk out. Once we eat, we are going to take you someplace where there are people you can rob." T.J. wasn't so bright and neither was his plan. I came up with an alternate plan to get away from them. All I had to do was use my pickpocketing skills to take the gun away from him. As soon as he and Bebe let go of my arms, that's what I had planned to do.

We walked toward Family Dollar, and I noticed that there were two police cruisers sitting in the parking lot. The three drug addicts must have still been partially high because they didn't even notice the police. Their only goal was to rob the place of food and rush out. Bebe and T.J. let go of my arms once we walked inside the store. I pushed them away and ran out the door. I thought for sure T.J. would run out of the store and shoot at me, but he didn't. I ran a safe distance away and then turned to see if they were following me. What I saw next made me stop cold. The three of them ran out of Family Dollar with bags of chips and snacks. They had not noticed that the police were in the store. Four cops chased them and easily tackled them to the ground. LaShaunda screamed out obscenities at the top of her voice. T.J. puked and Bebe tried to resist being handcuffed. More police showed up, and before long, they were taken away.

Once the police activity ended, I began walking. I didn't dare go back to the abandoned house to retrieve what few items of clothing I had hastily grabbed. It wasn't worth running into the other three zombies who had left earlier. I was cold, alone and in a strange city. I didn't know where I was headed. I only knew that I had to keep moving. I came across the McDonald's that T.J. had mentioned. I walked inside and searched for the bathroom. The people inside looked at me and cast judgment upon me. Their eyes said that I was a degenerate, immoral and the scum of society. I didn't think I was any of those things, but their eyes told a different story. I walked into the bathroom and locked the door. I looked at myself in the mirror and was horrified at my reflection. I had no idea how I'd gotten so dirty so quickly. My hair was a mess, my skin had dirty smudges on it and my top had black grime on it. I must have gotten the filth on me when I sat against the wall. I tried not to touch anything in the house, but I must have and then unconsciously touched my face. I turned on the water and snatched several paper towels from the dispenser. I wet them and squirted a healthy amount of hand soap on them. I cleaned myself as best as I could and then walked out.

I wandered around the streets for hours replaying the events of the day over and over in my mind. I tried to make

sense of everything. I tried to understand my crazy ratio-
nale for following LaShaunda to her personal hell. I tried
to understand why I felt so alone, so hopeless and so un-
loved. I didn't have a single answer to any of my questions.

I had been walking aimlessly for so long that I had not
noticed that the sun had set. Nightfall was less than thirty
minutes away, and I had no place to sleep. I had no blanket,
no warm clothes, no bed, no money and no phone. I looked
toward the heavens when I heard the rumble of thunder and
flashes of lightning crack across the horizon. A few minutes later, the sky opened up and it rained hard and heavy. I
shivered and trembled because I was so cold and wet. I came
to a church and pulled on the door. I thought I would be
able to go inside and get warm, but the doors were locked.
I continued on to a place called Mitchell Park. There was
an overpass there, and I took shelter from the rain under
it. I sat at the highest point of the sloped concrete, pulled
my knees to my chest and hugged myself to keep warm.
I prayed. I prayed to the angels. I prayed to my father and
asked him for help, strength and guidance. I was tired but
I knew that falling asleep beneath an expressway overpass
was out of the question.

The next morning I crawled from beneath the overpass
and continued walking. I was hungry and had to get food
from somewhere. It was still drizzling and the temperature
had dropped to around the high thirties. My breath formed
clouded puffs that lingered. Then the strangest thing happened. A very odd feeling washed over me, and I stood very
still. The wind blew and it was no longer cold, but warm
instead. In my mind I heard the voice of an old man pleading with me to call home. The voice sounded familiar, as if I
knew the person, but I had no idea who the voice belonged

to. The voice and the feeling disappeared as quickly as they had arrived. I thought my mind was playing tricks on me.

"Young lady, do you need help?"

I was startled out of my daydream. A policeman was standing in front of me.

"Huh?" I asked.

"Do you need help? It's cold out here, and you don't have on a coat." The police officer was a tall Mexican man in his fifties who had eyes that looked familiar. They were sharp and distinguished, like eagle eyes. I suddenly remembered why his eyes were so recognizable. There was an old photo of my grandfather sitting on Grandmother Esmeralda's dresser. I had looked at the photo countless times. I looked more deeply into the eyes of the policeman. It was bizarre how much he looked like the photo of my grandfather in his military uniform. I had never met my grandfather because he passed away before I was born, but this man reminded me of him. I don't know why I thought about my grandfather at that moment, but I couldn't stop thinking about him and the stories my grandmother had told me about him.

"Why don't you come inside the station with me? I'll fix you some hot chocolate so you can get warm," he suggested.

"Station?" My mind was still trying to clear away the fog.

"Right here." The officer nodded in the direction of the station I was standing in front of.

"May I use the phone inside, to call home?" I asked.

"Yes," he said and took off his long black raincoat and draped it over my shoulders.

twenty-five

MAYA

MY house and world had been turned upside down. Viviana had been missing for two days, and no one knew if she was alive or dead. We didn't know if she had been kidnapped or met some other horrible fate. My heart was filled with guilt and regret. I should not have shown the video to my mother. In my heart I knew that Viviana's disappearance was related to my telltale heart. My big mouth had once again caused a major family crisis, and I felt awful.

Grandmother Esmeralda had spent countless hours praying, but her prayers for Viviana's return had not been answered. It was time to call the police. My aunt Salena, Viviana's mother, had been contacted and was on her way. Keysha and her family took the time to print missing person's flyers and were out posting them.

Grandmother Esmeralda, Anna, Paul, my mother and I were sitting at the kitchen table. My father, who was standing nearby, held the cordless phone in his hand. He was about to dial the police department when my cell phone rang. I removed it from my hip holster and saw that it was a call from the 414 area code.

"Who is that?" asked my father.

"I don't know. It's probably a wrong number. It's from

the four-fourteen area code. I don't know where that is or anyone from there."

"Answer the phone, Maya!" Grandmother Esmeralda urged me.

"Hello," I answered, but no one said a word. All I heard was a bunch of noise in the background.

"Hello," I spoke again. I looked at my family and shrugged my shoulders. I was confused.

I pressed the speakerphone feature so everyone could hear and spoke a third time. "Hello," I said.

"Hello. Is anyone there?" a man's voice asked.

"Who is this?" I asked.

"This is Officer Fernando from the Milwaukee Police Department. I have a young lady here who was wandering the streets. She looked very lost and afraid, so I asked her if she needed any help. She asked if she could use the phone, and she dialed this number."

"Is it Viviana?" my grandmother asked.

"Is your name Viviana?" I heard him ask. "She's nodding her head yes," said Officer Fernando.

"Oh, thank You, God!" cried out Grandmother Esmeralda. "Thank You, thank You, thank You."

"She looks very tired and like she has seen better days. Does she have any type of medical condition?" asked Officer Fernando.

"No," Grandmother Esmeralda spoke. "Could you please give us your address so that we can come get her?"

A few days later, once the chaos had settled down, Grandmother Esmeralda sat down with me and Viviana. She claimed that something was heavy on her heart, and she needed to discuss it with us. I figured she was going to grill

Viviana about why she had run away to Milwaukee and how she had ended up at the police station. When we picked her up, my mother began asking Viviana those types of questions, but Grandmother Esmeralda put a stop to my mother's interrogation. The three of us sat at the kitchen table. I was silent and so was Viviana.

"What is going on between you two?" she asked, but neither Viviana nor I spoke.

"Come on. Tell me. The hostility you have toward each other is unmistakable," Grandmother Esmeralda said. Viviana and I remained silent. "Okay, since you two will not talk, you will listen." She paused, then cleared her throat. "There is a curse on the family."

"A what?" I broke the silence.

"A curse, Maya, and it's nothing to play with or make fun of." Grandmother Esmeralda gazed at me with an intensity that I'd never seen before.

"Were you someplace dark and evil?" Grandmother Esmeralda asked Viviana.

Twisting her lip, Viviana answered slowly. "Yes. It felt like that." Grandmother Esmeralda made the sign of the cross and said a quick prayer.

"The curse on the family comes from your grandfather. When he came home from the war, he said that he felt a demon on him."

"Seriously? Is this conversation necessary?" Viviana appeared to be annoyed. Grandmother Esmeralda slapped her palm against the table and raised her voice.

"Yes. It is very necessary. Listen to what I am saying. Your grandfather, may God rest his soul, was a good soldier. He fought for the country in the Vietnam War, and it was a nightmare for him. He said that he felt like he had gone to hell. He was forced to do bad things that went against his Christian beliefs. He had to break up families, snatch children from the arms of their fathers and kill them. If he had not killed the men, they would have come back and ambushed their camp. He always talked about how horrible the fighting was. Death, destruction and evil were all around him.

"After the war ended and he came home, he had horrible nightmares. A demon came to visit him and told him that his family would be cursed for generations, and that there would never be harmony and happiness. Your grandfather took this as a sign. He interpreted it to mean that his family would always go through some type of hell. When Raven and Salena were born, he gave them all the love he had. He wanted his family to love each other and be strong for each other. Sadly, this was not the case. Raven and Salena fought all the time. They never got along well. I believe that the evil spirit that followed your grandfather home is responsible for all of the animosity between Raven and Salena. Now that same evil spirit has pitted you and Maya against each other."

"I don't feel like there is a demon following me," I said, swiveling my head in disbelief.

"That's because the demon has clouded your vision. I have to help you both see. It is the only way you will be able to break this horrible curse and end your feuding. You're fighting with each other, and it has gotten nasty. I know this to be true because Anna has told me about it. Viviana, you're mad at Maya because she told the police about your father. Because of what Maya said, your father went to jail and was murdered. Instead of accepting the fact that your father was a bad man, it is easier for you to fill your heart with hatred and evil toward Maya. That's how the demon works. He plays tricks on your mind.

"Viviana, your father was a bad man. He hurt people, people feared him and he took a life. That is the truth. It is also true that your father, when he was a boy, was very gifted. I believe that your father gave the best of who he was to you. You are gifted just like he was, but he made bad choices in life and wasted the gift. If you truly want to honor your father's memory, then use the gift he passed on to you. Don't let the demon trick you into filling your heart with evil toward Maya because she did the right thing." Grandmother Esmeralda paused for a moment to allow her words to sink in. I noticed that Viviana smeared away tears. I suddenly felt my heart fill up with sympathy, and I could not understand why.

"And, Maya, you need to have more compassion. Viviana has suffered a great loss. When a little girl loses her father, it leaves a big empty hole in her heart. You have no right to make her feel as if she is beneath you. You have no right to attack her self-esteem or the unfortunate events in her life. You could learn a lot from her. She's very strong and smarter than you think she is."

"I believe you. I believe everything you've just said." Viviana's voice trembled. "This may sound strange, but right before the police found me, a voice told me to call home. I had never heard the voice before, but I recognized it. Then the policeman who found me had eyes like Granpa."

"Yes. I noticed that, too, about Officer Fernando. Now that you've shared that with me, I can tell you that your grandfather was with you. He was probably with you when you decided to try and walk through hell. He helped you find your way out. That's love, Viviana. He was guiding you away from danger. He did not want the demon to take your soul to hell."

"Why did you call my cell phone number and not the house line or Grandmother Esmeralda?" I asked. Viviana looked deeply into my eyes.

"A voice in my head told me to call you and I did," she answered.

"That was your grandfather. He wants you two to stop fighting and love each other," Grandmother Esmeralda said.

I don't know what came over me in that moment, but I had to exhale to keep my emotions from overwhelming me.

"I'm sorry," I said, looking down at my lap and then at Viviana. "I'm sorry for making you feel unwelcome. I am actually very happy that you're here, and I was only being mean because you were being mean to me."

Viviana did something I didn't expect. She said nothing. Instead she stood up, walked over to me, leaned into me, hugged me and cried.

twenty-six

VIVIANA

"Are you okay?" Maya asked me.

"Yes. I have not felt this good in a very long time," I said to her as we walked toward Tinley Park High School. We had just arrived for another competition.

"Are you ready?" Keysha asked as she walked alongside me. She held the door open for me, and I walked through. Misalo and Red were behind us, talking to Mr. Morgan. So much had changed in my life since Grandmother Esmeralda helped Maya and I work through our differences. Grandmother Esmeralda was right. I resented and even hated Maya for snitching on my father, but in my heart, I knew that she only did what was right. Grandmother Esmeralda told me and Maya that doing the right thing sometimes hurts and that doing the right thing sometimes is not the best thing.

"Following military orders was the right thing for your grandfather to do, but it wasn't the best thing for his soul. Maya did the right thing by telling the truth about your father, Viviana, but it wasn't the best thing for your mother and father because he ended up in jail. Your mother leaving you with Raven and Maya was the right thing to do because she couldn't provide you with a stable home, but it wasn't the best thing for you emotionally. Life is not easy, but as long as you have love and family, it's well worth living," she had said after Maya and I had stopped crying long enough to apologize to each other.

My father was very smart, academically, when he was younger, but he made a choice and got involved with and eventually became the leader of a well-known street gang. As a little girl, I was in denial, and in my mind I had created a version of him that was likable and less threatening. Perhaps in some unexplainable way he did pass along the best of who he was to me, and I thank him for that.

"Is your friend, LaShaunda, coming?" asked Misalo as he walked past.

"I don't think so," I said. Misalo smiled at me and gave me a fist bump. He was still hard to resist and handsome. I had promised Maya that I would no longer tempt him and told her that, if she ever messed up with him, I would beat her down. I did hear back from LaShaunda. She called me from the detention center where she was being held until her court date. She was unapologetic when I asked her why she had set me up. She didn't even want to talk about it. She only wanted to discuss her court date and how much fun she and T.J. were going to have when she got out. She said that they would find a new place to hang out and live day by day. It was then that the friendship blinders I had been wearing had come completely off. LaShaunda didn't want to take ownership of her actions, and she believed the lifestyle T.J. offered her was a reasonable one.

"What's up, Team Captain?" Red walked up and hugged me.

"A murder charge if you ever put your hands on me again." I quickly removed his hands. Red had been trying to create romance where none existed. He liked me more than I liked him.

"It's good to have you back on the team, Viviana," Mr. Morgan said as we entered the auditorium. "Making a solid commitment to the team was the right thing to do."

"Thanks for letting me come back," I said. I proudly walked onto the stage with my team. The entire team had spent several days studying with each other for this competition. Tinley Park High was ranked number one, and due to my absence, we had slipped down to number three. I was ready to change all of that when I stepped behind the podium. As I waited for the round to begin, I glanced out in the audience and noticed that Uncle Herman, Aunt Raven, Anna, Paul, Grandmother Esmeralda and my mother were all there to support us. My heart got full when I saw all of them smiling. Maya was standing next to me. I leaned over and gave her a hug.

"What was that for?" Maya asked.

"Let's just say that being homeless for two days taught me a valuable lesson," I said.

"And what lesson would that be?" Maya asked.

"To appreciate those who mean the most to me," I said and noticed that Maya's eyes filled with emotion. I knew that she was happy that our feud had been completely squashed. The moderator asked if we were ready. We all said yes. I placed my trigger thumb on top of the buzzer and waited for the question.

"What year did African and Islamic Moors take over Spain?"

I pressed the buzzer first. "Seven hundred thirty-one and they ruled until the year 1492 when Queen Isabella reached an agreement with them. Once Spain was free, Queen Isabella was able to send Christopher Columbus on his voyage to the Americas."

"That is a correct and very thorough answer," the moderator said.

"I'm on fire today. Next question," I said, smiling confidently.

★ ★ ★ ★ ★

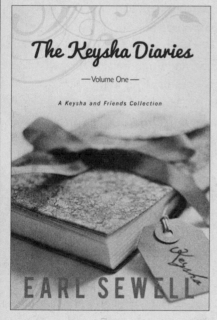

WITH FAMILY LIKE THIS, WHO NEEDS ENEMIES?

BACK TO ME

A KEYSHA AND FRIENDS NOVEL

Earl Sewell

Maya Rogers had hoped to get famous…but not this way. First her boyfriend, Misalo, dumps her, and then the revealing photos that she sent to him go viral. How did life get so out of control so fast? One answer: Viviana, Maya's estranged cousin. Viviana is stirring up lots of trouble. At least Maya knows that her best friend Keysha always has her back. But with so much bad blood flowing, will these family ties be severed for good?

"Sewell addresses some major social issues that confront young adults in a way that is both satisfying and nonthreatening." —*School Library Journal* on *MYSELF AND I*

Available now wherever books are sold.

www.Harlequin.com

KPCON4630512TR-F

KPAA464021 2TR-R